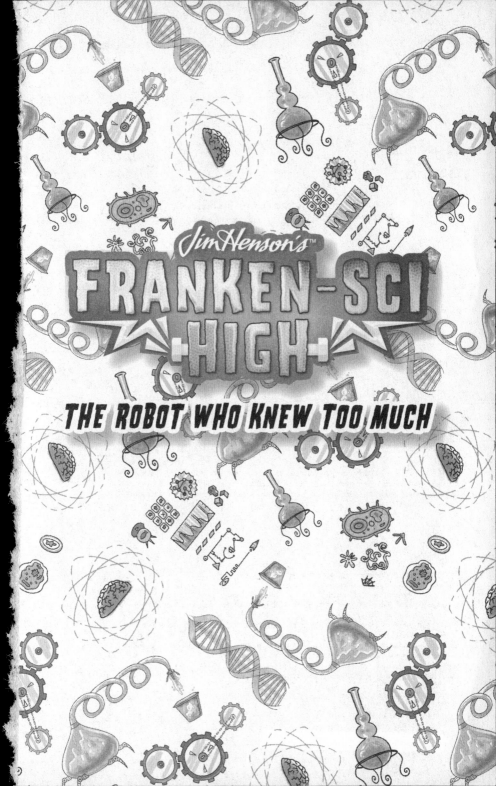

Jim Henson's™
FRANKEN-SCI HIGH

THE ROBOT WHO KNEW TOO MUCH

As a child, seeing you create
tiny worlds inspired me to create my own.
This one is for you, Mom. —M. Y.

SIMON SPOTLIGHT
An imprint of Simon & Schuster Children's Publishing Division
1230 Avenue of the Americas, New York, New York 10020
This Simon Spotlight hardcover edition April 2020
© 2020 The Jim Henson Company
JIM HENSON'S mark & logo, FRANKEN-SCI HIGH mark & logo, characters, and elements are trademarks of The Jim Henson Company. All Rights Reserved.
All rights reserved, including the right of reproduction in whole or in part in any form.
SIMON SPOTLIGHT and colophon are registered trademarks of Simon & Schuster, Inc.
For information about special discounts for bulk purchases, please contact Simon & Schuster Special Sales at 1-866-506-1949 or business@simonandschuster.com.
Designed by Ciara Gay
Manufactured in the United States of America 0320 FFG
10 9 8 7 6 5 4 3 2 1
ISBN 978-1-4814-9137-2 (hc)
ISBN 978-1-4814-9136-5 (pbk)
ISBN 978-1-4814-9138-9 (eBook)

Jim Henson's™ FRANKEN-SCI HIGH

THE ROBOT WHO KNEW TOO MUCH

CREATED BY **MARK YOUNG**
TEXT WRITTEN BY **TRACEY WEST**
ILLUSTRATED BY **MARIANO EPELBAUM**

Simon Spotlight
New York London Toronto Sydney New Delhi

CHAPTER 1

The Future Is Funky

A lot of strange things had happened to Newton Warp since the day he'd appeared at Franken-Sci High with no memories at all.

That was the first strange thing—not knowing who he was. He had a student ID that said his name was Newton Warp and that he was a student at the school. But that's all he knew. And nobody at the school could tell him who he was, not even the professors or the headmistress, Ms. Mumtaz.

The other strange things had happened very quickly, one after another. He met his roommate, who was a talking mound of green goo. His best friends were a robot, and a girl who rescued monsters. Then Newton discovered that he had some unusual powers, such as sticky fingers and toes, and the ability to camouflage himself.

Other strange things had happened too, but at the

moment, Newton was thinking that what had *just* happened was really, truly bizarre and confusing. His friend Shelly Ravenholt, the monster rescuer, was thinking the same thing.

They were standing in the school gym, facing Professor Flubitus, a green-haired man wearing a polka-dot shirt, shiny black pants, yellow boots, a vest with blinking LED lights, and a red bow tie.

It wasn't just his outfit that was strange, but what he'd told them. He had said that he had traveled all the way from the future to protect Newton and Shelly.

"*Your* future," he specified. "I'm afraid it's not looking so good."

Newton and Shelly stood there with their mouths open for a few long seconds. Then Higgy, Newton's gooey roommate (he was made of protoplasm, actually), spoke up.

"How *not good* do you mean?" he asked. "Not good, like how eating a sandwich with stale crusts is not good? Or how movies with talking babies are not good? Or more of a funky not good, like really stinky cheese?"

"I *like* movies with talking babies," muttered Theremin, Newton's robot friend.

Professor Flubitus frowned. "Far worse than funky, I am afraid," he said.

Newton finally spoke. "Mumtaz told us that you were following us around to protect us. Protect us from what?" he asked, his voice rising. "What is going to happen?"

"I'm afraid I can't tell you that," Flubitus said, his face turning as red as his bow tie. "If I did that, it might alter the future. That's one of the first rules of time travel, you know."

Shelly snapped out of her stunned trance. "Who's making these rules, exactly?" she asked.

Then they heard Ms. Mumtaz's voice behind them.

"Flubitus, what's going on here?" she asked. "What happened to the monster?"

The monster—that was another strange thing that had happened recently. During a family reunion, Shelly had helped out a small blue creature called a Transylvanian baccatrei. The grateful monster, Peewee, had followed Shelly to the school without her knowing it. Professor Flubitus had found Peewee trying to get into the school, and had brought him inside.

Before Flubitus could return the creature to Shelly, Peewee had eaten a nanochip that had transformed him into a giant, three-eyed, fire-breathing monster with spikes on his head. Professor Flubitus had deactivated the chip and returned Peewee to his normal state. But he

was no hero as far as Newton was concerned. Because Flubitus had confessed that the nanochip had been intended for Newton!

Shelly held up Peewee and showed Mumtaz. "Here's the monster, back to normal," Shelly explained. "Professor Flubitus told us that Peewee ate a nanochip that turned him into the monster."

"A nanochip meant for *me*," Newton said. "Professor Flubitus was going to turn me into a monster."

"To protect you, my dear boy," Flubitus said.

"Protect me from what?" Newton asked. He turned to Ms. Mumtaz. "Why can't you tell us?"

The headmistress stared at him with small, bright eyes that reminded Newton of a bird. Her thin, pointy nose and orange-and-purple-streaked hair added to her avian appearance.

"Newton, the members of the faculty have been keeping a secret from you," she said. "Professor Flubitus came from the future to warn us that the school will be in great danger, and you are our only hope."

Our only hope. The words felt big and scary to Newton. *Am I really that important?* he wondered.

"I can't tell you any more than that," Mumtaz continued. "Or it would be disastrous to the space-time continuum."

"That sounds *extra* funky," Higgy remarked.

"I don't understand," Newton said. "Earlier you told me and Shelly that Professor Flubitus was keeping an eye on us. So why am *I* the only hope and not both of us?"

Flubitus turned red again. "It's . . . uh . . . well . . . I simply can't tell you! You'll just have to trust me!"

"Can I trust you to not try to turn me into a fire-breathing monster again?" Newton asked.

The professor looked at Ms. Mumtaz, as though he hoped she would give him permission to try again.

"He absolutely will *not* be trying to turn you into a monster again," the headmistress said firmly. "Isn't that right, Flubitus?"

The professor nodded energetically. "That's right. No more monster transformations. We will just have to hope that Newton's own—"

A sharp look from Mumtaz stopped him from saying anything more. She turned to Newton. "I know this is a lot to take in, Newton, but you have to take my word for it. Flubitus is on your side."

"But how do you know he's even telling you the truth about the future?" Newton pressed her. "He's the only one who witnessed it, right?"

"We have no reason to doubt Professor Flubitus,"

Ms. Mumtaz said. "I need you to believe us, Newton. And I need you to just go on with your life and forget about all this future business, if you can. Just let the future unfold."

"And then what?" Newton asked. "If something bad happens to the school, what am I supposed to do?"

"You'll know what to do when the time comes," she promised him.

I want to believe her, Newton thought. *But it's hard to when she won't give me any more details. Still, do I have a choice?*

Ms. Mumtaz gazed at Flubitus and the students. "It's late. I suggest you all get back to your dorms. Shelly, please put Peewee with the rest of your animals."

"Yes, Ms. Mumtaz," Shelly said, and the headmistress turned and left the gym, her heels clacking on the floor as she went.

"I'll go with you, Shelly," Theremin offered.

"Me too," Newton said.

"I need to grab a snack," Higgy said. "Catch you later!"

Newton turned to Professor Flubitus. "I get that you're trying to protect us, but could you please stop following us?" he asked. "It's creepy."

"It is my sworn duty to protect you," the professor

7

said, and then he tripped over his own feet. The kids were used to his clumsiness by now, so they tried to ignore it.

"I think we've been doing a pretty good job of protecting ourselves," Newton said.

"That's right!" Theremin piped up. "Newton and Shelly have me to protect them! Do you have super robot strength? Can you shoot lasers out of your eyes?"

"Er, no," Flubitus replied.

"So you don't have to worry about us," Theremin said. "Come on, guys, let's go!"

Theremin zoomed off, floating above the ground on his hover legs, and Newton and Shelly followed on foot.

"That was impressive, Theremin," Shelly said. "I hope you convinced Flubitus to give us some space. Newton's right—it was creepy having him follow us around like that."

They made their way to the basement of the school, where Shelly had an animal rescue lab. They were all animals that Shelly had found on the island who needed a little help. Wingold the parrot had one robotic wing. There was a frog with springs to replace some missing legs, a turtle with a titanium shell, and a lizard with wheels for feet. Plants kept alive by artificial sunlight helped re-create the animals' island habitat.

Shelly placed Peewee on a tree branch.

"Here's your new home, Peewee," she told him.

The tiny blue creature looked at her with big, sad eyes.

"Don't worry. You'll see me twice a day, when it's feeding time," she said. The little creature squeaked and then curled up for a nap.

Shelly sighed. "Poor little guy," she said. "He was lost and alone when I found him, and scared. I could bring him back to Transylvania and let him loose, but that doesn't feel right. I'd want to find his family first."

Lost, alone, and scared. Newton had felt the same way when Shelly and Theremin had found him in the school's Brain Bank just a couple of months ago. When Newton, Shelly, and Theremin won the school's Mad Science Fair and each received a portal pass as a prize, Newton tried to use it to find his family. The portal pass was supposed to be able to take you anywhere you wanted to go, but when he asked it to take him home, nothing happened. He stayed right there in the school. That experience had left him with a longing, wondering if he'd ever know who his family was, and if he had a family at all.

Thank goodness I have my friends, he thought, and he smiled at Shelly.

"Peewee was lucky that he found you," he said. "And I guess I was too."

"I think Theremin and I are the lucky ones," Shelly said. "This place has gotten a lot better since you showed up."

"That's right," Theremin agreed. "We won the science fair together. You saved me from being sucked into a black hole. You made it snow in my room. You're the best, Newton."

"Thanks," Newton said. "You guys are making me feel funny. Like, I've got this warm, fuzzy feeling."

Theremin's eyes glowed, and he scanned Newton. "Your endorphin levels are elevated," he reported.

"That just means you're happy," Shelly explained.

Newton grinned. Things at Franken-Sci High were strange, and weird, and unusual, but they were pretty good, too.

"Yeah, I guess I am happy," he replied.

The three friends left the animal rescue lab and headed upstairs and outside the main school building. A blast of warm, humid tropical air hit Newton's face as they walked down the jungle path to the student dorms. Newton and Theremin said good night to Shelly and went inside the boys' dorm. Theremin made his way to his room, and Newton went to the room he shared with Higgy.

He opened the door, expecting to find Higgy awake. But the lights were out, and his roommate was snoring in the bottom bunk. Newton froze.

Higgy loved to play pranks on Newton, and by now Newton knew to look out for them. He scanned the room—thanks to his special abilities, he could see perfectly in the dark. Everything looked normal, with Higgy's clothes piled messily on the floor, and empty candy bar and chip wrappers strewn about. He quietly walked to the bunk bed and used his grippy fingertips to pull himself up to the top bunk. The bed was empty. Satisfied, Newton came back down. He kicked off his sneakers and changed into a T-shirt and shorts to sleep in. Then he scrambled to the top bunk, stretched out, and rested his head on the pillow.

Pfffffffffffffft!

The farting sound came from beneath the pillow. Newton lifted it up and found a rubber chicken underneath!

"Very funny, Higgy," Newton said. "That's pretty lame, though, compared to some of your pranks."

Suddenly a disco ball dropped down from the ceiling. Music with a heavy beat blared through the dorm room. And next to Newton, the rubber chicken started moving! It stood on two legs and hopped off the top

bunk. Then it danced underneath the disco lights.

Higgy peeked out from the bottom bunk. "Pretty cool, huh? I had to rework the standard reanimation formula to have it work on a rubber chicken, and they're not very smart. But it only took me three days to teach it how to dance!"

"You went to all that trouble just to prank me?" Newton asked.

"Of course I did," Higgy replied. "And it was totally worth it."

Newton gazed at the rubber chicken, shaking its chicken behind to the music and flapping its wings up and down. A word popped into his mind.

"Would you call this a *funky* chicken?" Newton asked.

"Exactly, roomie!" Higgy said. He slid out of his bunk and started to wiggle along with the chicken. "Do the funky chicken!"

Newton hopped down from the top bunk and joined them.

"There you go, Newton!" Higgy cried. "Flap those chicken wings!"

Newton laughed. *Maybe the future's going to be bad,* he thought. *But now . . . now is pretty awesome.* Then he happily joined Higgy in a disco move.

CHAPTER 2

Fun with Frankenstein

The next morning Newton stopped in front his locker, number 325.17. He pressed his finger to a button on the locker's glass pad. *Beep!* Next he opened his eyes wide for the eye scan. *Beep!* Finally, cringing with anticipation, he licked the taste-sensitive security lines for the saliva analysis.

"Mmm," he said. "Banana . . . blue cheese?" He wrinkled his nose.

Shelly and Theremin approached him. "I think today's flavor is very unfair," Shelly remarked. "You think you're safe with the banana, and then, yuck!"

"I have no idea what either of those things tastes like, but when you guys talk about it, it makes me glad I don't produce saliva," Theremin said.

Newton sniffed the air. "Maybe some food is gross, but bacon is amazing," he said. "I wish you could taste bacon, Theremin. Maybe your dad could

install some taste sensors for you."

At the mention of his dad, Theremin's eyes flashed.

"I don't think my father wants to do me any favors," he said.

Newton felt bad. Theremin's dad, Dr. Rozika, was a professor at the school and had wanted Theremin to be smart, but not smarter than him. So anytime Theremin got really good at something, he automatically failed at something else. Sometimes the professor said it was for Theremin's own good, but it only made Theremin miserable.

"Right, Theremin," Newton said. "Bad idea. Sorry I mentioned it."

"It's cool," Theremin said, to Newton's relief. Then the three friends took the glass transport tube to the school cafeteria.

When the doors opened, Newton saw the word "bacon" flash on the digital menu board on the buffet line.

"Yay!" he cheered, and he hurried toward the line, with Shelly behind him. He picked up a plate and held it up to the blue-haired cafeteria worker.

"Bacon, please," he said.

The woman dropped a small, brown capsule onto Newton's plate with a pair of tongs. Newton stared at it.

"Is this a new kind of bacon?" he asked.

"It's something they cooked up in the food lab," she replied cheerfully. "It's got all the calories and fat of three pieces of bacon, with none of the fuss or the grease."

Shelly popped her capsule into her mouth and frowned. "Or the taste."

Newton swallowed his bacon capsule and frowned. "This is very sad," he said.

The cafeteria worker lowered her voice. "Yes, we've been getting a lot of complaints," she said. "But as the old mad-scientist motto goes: 'Some experiments succeed, and some fail!'"

Shelly grabbed Newton by the elbow. "Come on, let's get smoothies," she said.

"I'll save us a table," Theremin offered, and he zoomed off.

Disappointed by the bacon capsules, many kids were already in the smoothie line. Newton realized that when he'd first shown up at the school, everybody had been a stranger to him. But now he knew almost everyone.

At the head of the line, Mimi Crowninshield was boasting to Gustav Goddard.

"Crowninshield Enterprises is the leading innovator in stealth technology," she was saying. "My parents have a machine that can make the moon disappear!"

"Doesn't that happen once a month anyway?" Gustav asked, and Mimi scowled.

Behind them, Tori Twitcher filled a glass with coconut milk, and Newton remembered that on his first day at Franken-Sci High, Theremin had seen her acting like a cat at Nurse Bunsen's office because of a mind-control accident. Today she was acting like a regular human.

Next in line was Tootie Van der Flootin, master monster maker. She wore her hair in a bun on top of her head, as usual.

Behind her stood a tall, greasy-haired teenager, Rotwang. While most of the students in the school were descended from the world's greatest mad scientists, Rotwang came from a long line of mad-scientist assistants.

The mad scientist he served, Odifin Pinkwad, was a brain in a jar of fluid who got around on a small table with wheels, pushed by Rotwang. Odifin's voice came out of a speaker on the jar.

"Rotwang, why are we waiting in this infernal line?" Odifin complained.

"I'm hungry, boss!" Rotwang replied.

"What an inconvenience," Odifin scoffed. "So much time wasted with your bodily needs. The next thing you

know, you'll want to waste more of my time brushing your teeth!"

Then Odifin spun around, or at least his brain did, in the jar. "Who is that invading my perimeter?"

An orange tentacle had poked out of the pocket of Tootie's lab coat. She was now at the front of the line, and the tentacle had stretched past Rotwang and was tapping on Odifin's jar. Tootie reeled in the tentacle as if it was fishing line and stuffed it back into her pocket, which she had adapted to be extra large.

"Sorry, Odifin," Tootie said. "Just a new monster creation I'm working on." Then she pressed some buttons on the smoothie machine and turned to Newton and Shelly.

"Hey, guys," she said as she picked up her glass. "How's Peewee doing, Shelly?"

"He's back to his normal, cute little self," Shelly answered.

Tootie frowned. "That's good, I guess. But I thought he was pretty cute when he was a giant, three-eyed, fire-breathing monster."

Shelly grinned. "I don't think you ever met a monster you didn't like, Tootie! And you know I'm the same way. . . ."

The orange tentacle snuck out of Tootie's pocket

again. It grabbed the smoothie glass from Tootie's hand and retreated. Tootie smiled.

"Looks like little Octavius is thirsty," she said.

Tootie moved on, and soon it was Newton and Shelly's turn to make their smoothies.

Newton never really cared what his smoothies tasted like, so he pressed random buttons on the digital screen. *Kale. Pineapple. Protein Powder. Cod Liver Oil. Jalapeño. Persimmon. Cucumber. Brain-Boosting Vitamins.*

When he finished, thick, green sludge poured into his glass. Newton sipped it as he and Shelly walked to meet Theremin at their table.

"How does yours taste?" she asked, grimacing.

Newton took another sip. "Like . . . not bacon," he answered, and Shelly laughed.

As they took their seats, three loud beeps sounded across the cafeteria. Then the giant holographic head and torso of Headmistress Mumtaz appeared in the center of the room.

"Good morning, students of Franken-Sci High," she began. "As you know, each year we enrich our science curriculum by turning to the arts, in the form of our annual school play. This year it's extra special, because we're going to be celebrating the two hundredth anniversary of our great school."

Everyone let out a cheer.

"In honor of that milestone, I am pleased to announce that our theatrical performance will be *Frankenstein: The Musical*, in honor of one of the most famous mad scientists of all time, Victor Frankenstein!"

A murmur rippled through the cafeteria. Everyone started talking and whispering excitedly, and Newton wondered what the big deal was.

"Auditions will be held Thursday, after the final class period," Mumtaz went on. "A list of available roles has been sent to your tablets."

Her hologram disappeared, and students scrambled to look at their tablets to see what parts they could audition for.

"Can you guys remind me who this Frankenstein guy was, again?" Newton asked.

"Ask Shelly," Theremin said. "She's related to the Frankensteins."

"Really?" Newton asked.

"Yes," Shelly said. "Victor Frankenstein was, like, the first famous mad scientist. He had a book written about him, and it got made into a bunch of movies. But they got a lot of the story wrong. In the book and the movies he dies, but that's not what really happened."

"What did happen?" Newton asked.

"While searching for the monster he created, Victor Frankenstein ended up here, in the Bermuda Triangle," Shelly replied. "He got married and had a bunch of kids. My great-great-great-great-great-granddad was one of them. But then, about one hundred years ago, there was a family feud at a wedding. One branch of the family was so upset that they changed their name from Frankenstein to Ravenholt. They left the islands and moved to Transylvania."

"You should try out for the play, Shelly," Theremin said. "Since you're really a Frankenstein, you'd be perfect!"

Shelly frowned. "I don't know. I have mixed feelings about it. My family has distanced ourselves from the Frankensteins for so long. I don't know how my parents would feel about it."

"I guess I understand," Newton said. "I just have one more question. What's a play?"

"Your memory banks amaze me," Theremin said. "It's fascinating how you know some things and not others."

Newton shrugged. "I think it's more annoying than fascinating."

Shelly piped up. "To answer your question, a play is when people act out a story for entertainment. And

a musical is when they spontaneously burst into song while they're telling the story."

Newton frowned. "Spontaneously burst into song? Does that happen in real life?"

"Almost never," Shelly replied. "But when you're watching a musical, you don't think about that. It feels right."

"Hmm," Newton said, feeling curious. He opened up his tablet, and read the announcement about the play auditions.

GOOD MORNING, PROSPECTIVE THESPIANS!

I, Professor Snollygoster, have the great honor of directing this year's theatrical performance: **Frankenstein: The Musical.**

When casting the roles, I am not searching for someone who looks like a character. The actor portraying each part should have, or be able to portray, the soul and spirit of whomever they are portraying. Therefore, the roles shall not be determined by age, gender, or appearance.

Please read these character descriptions before determining which role you will try out for. Select the character's name to be taken to a sample script page.

Dr. Frankenstein: a brilliant, misunderstood genius who wants to make the world a better place.

The Monster: lost and confused, the Monster struggles to find where he belongs in the world.

Igor, the Assistant: completely loyal and subservient to Dr. Frankenstein.

The bell announcing it was time for the next class stopped Newton from reading the rest of the parts. As he, Shelly, and Theremin made their way through the halls, he mulled over what he had read.

Lost and confused, Newton thought. *Maybe I should try out for this play. I have the soul and spirit of the Monster!*

They walked into the Genetic Friendgineering classroom, with Professor Thaddeus Wells. As usual, half of his body—a middle-aged man with a thin mustache and brown hair—was solid, while the other half looked fuzzy and constantly flickered in and out. An interdimensional portal accident had left the professor stuck between two dimensions.

"Good morning, students," Wells said from the solid side of his mouth. "I gather you are all excited about the play announcement this morning. I must say, you've got a better deal here. In the other dimension, they're doing something called *Mad-Scientist Roller Boogie 2: Disco Explosion*."

Tori Twitcher piped up. "I was really hoping we would do *Cats*. I'd love to play a cat."

"Maybe Snollygoster could add a role for you," Gustav suggested.

Mimi addressed the class. "Well, I, for one, think it's only fitting that we are honoring Dr. Frankenstein," she said. "And of course, I am the only one who deserves the role. We all know that I have the soul of a misunderstood genius!"

"Oh, we understand you, Mimi," Theremin said. "We understand that you don't have half the talent that Dr. Frankenstein had."

Mimi scowled. "Very funny, Theremin. What role are you going to try out for? Dr. Frankenstein's garbage can?"

"I have better things to do than try out for the play," Theremin replied. "And anyway, if anyone should play Dr. Frankenstein, it should be Shelly. She's actually related to him!"

"Well, just because you're some distant relative of Dr. Frankenstein doesn't mean you can act," Mimi said. "Because only the best actor will get the role. And that's going to be me!"

Newton thought about this. He had seen Mimi act

like she was being nice, when she was actually plotting something mean. If that was anything like acting in a play, he guessed that she'd be good at it.

Meanwhile, Shelly's eyes flashed, and she smiled. Newton knew Shelly well enough to know that she didn't back down from a challenge.

"I guess we'll find out on Thursday," Shelly told Mimi. "Because I'm trying out for the part of Dr. Frankenstein, and I'm going to get it!"

A few kids burst into applause.

"All right, class. Enough chatting," Professor Wells said. "There's a robot hamster on the loose in my other classroom, so I need you to settle down and take a pop quiz."

Boop! The first quiz question popped up on everyone's tablets, and the class quieted down. Newton read the first question.

True or false: Homozygous alleles may be dominant or recessive.

Now, Newton was a good student and had picked up a lot of knowledge in the few weeks that he'd been at the school. But he had a lot to catch up on, and it turns out that one of his strange abilities was useful in a situation like this. He leaned over to Shelly and whispered, "Can you say it?"

Shelly looked confused for a second, and then she nodded in understanding.

"Newton, use your noodle noggin," she whispered back.

Whoosh! It was like a closed door in his brain opened up, and information came flooding in.

"True," Newton said out loud while pressing *T* on his screen.

Correct!

He quickly blew through all twenty quiz questions, getting each one right. A little voice in his head worried that he was technically cheating, but he brushed it aside. He had amnesia, after all. Without the words "noodle noggin" triggering his memories, or maybe his intelligence, he'd fail every class. Besides, the answers were coming from his own brain.

Finishing early, he glanced over at Theremin.

Incorrect! flashed over and over on his screen. Newton felt bad for his friend.

After class the students spilled out into the hallway.

"That was some quiz," Newton said, glancing at Theremin.

"Yeah, I totally failed it," Theremin said. "But that was my plan. I've got a big programming test coming up, and I *can't* fail that. My dad is counting on me to ace it. So I've got to try to fail every quiz I have before the test. If I do well on the quizzes, my programming will kick in and I'll mess up the test."

"That's so unfair," Shelly said.

"I know," Theremin said. "But what can I do? I'm a Rozika, and Rozikas are programming geniuses. I've got to put all my energy toward this test. So I don't think I'm going to try out for the play. I'm going to be too busy studying."

"Isn't there some way that your dad could change your programming?" Newton wondered.

"No way," Theremin said.

"But did you ever ask him?" Newton asked. "I mean—"

"You don't know Father at all!" Theremin snapped, his eyes flashing red. Then he angrily zoomed away.

Newton sighed. "Sorry. I wish my noodle noggin could help me know how to be a better friend."

"You're a great friend, Newton," Shelly said. "Theremin's issues with his dad—they're complicated."

"I know," Newton said. *But there's got to be some way we can help him!* he thought.

CHAPTER 3

So Emotional

Over the next few days, all anyone talked about was the play. Kids practiced their roles in their rooms, in the hallways, and even standing on tables in the cafeteria. Finally Thursday came.

Newton had decided that he would try out for the Monster. Shelly was determined to play Dr. Frankenstein. And even Theremin had decided to audition.

"I'll try out for a small part," he said. "The Castle Cook, or something like that. If you guys are gonna be in it, I don't want to miss out."

They walked into the school auditorium. Onstage, a robot keyboard player, violinist, and drummer were warming up. Professor Snollygoster stood in front of the stage, facing the kids as they filed in. He was a tall man with an impressive swirl of blue-black hair on top of his head and bright blue eyes. Usually he wore a white lab coat over a white shirt and white pants, but

today he wore a black turtleneck and matching pants, and a black beret on his head.

"Take a seat, take a seat, everyone!" he said. "We are about to begin!"

Newton, Shelly, and Theremin slid into a row in the back of the auditorium. Newton scanned the rows in front of him and saw about forty kids wanting to try out.

The chattering quieted down, and Snollygoster cleared his throat. "I am very gratified to see such interest in this theatrical endeavor!" he said. "I see that most of you are auditioning for the major roles, and that is fine. Based on your performance, you may be assigned to a smaller role when all is cast. But of course, there are no small roles, really. Every role is an important one!"

"Ha!" Mimi snorted from her perch in the front row. "Everyone knows that the biggest roles are the best."

"On the contrary, Mimi, many actors have made a big splash with a small role," Snollygoster countered. "As a teacher of emotional chemistry, I can tell you that the key is *emotion*. Put your emotions into your role, and everyone will notice."

Newton started to feel a little nervous. He had read the audition part for the Monster on his tablet, and it seemed easy enough to memorize the words and say or sing them. He didn't know anything about putting *emotion* into it.

Snollygoster looked at his tablet. "We will begin with auditions for the Monster," he said. "And I see we only have one student signed up. Newton Warp, please come forward."

Stage fright washed over Newton, and he felt frozen in his chair. Then he felt Shelly nudge him.

"Newton! You're doing that thing," she whispered.

Newton looked down at himself, and saw that he had camouflaged himself to blend into the seat.

Snollygoster was peering into the dim auditorium with his hand over his eyes. "Newton? Are you here?"

Newton's fear of being found out as able to camouflage himself overtook his fear of auditioning, and he was able to revert to his usual self in a split second. "Here!" he replied. Then he squeezed past Theremin on his way out of the row.

"Break a leg, Newton!" Theremin said.

Newton stopped. "Why would you say such a thing?"

"It's a theater thing, but never mind," Theremin said. "Get up there! And don't be nervous!"

Don't camouflage! Don't camouflage! Newton told himself as he made his way to the stage. He stood in the

center and faced the kids in the seats. The bright stage lights made him squint.

"Let's begin with a bar from the song," Snollygoster said, and Newton nodded. He had practiced the song over and over in his dorm room. The robot orchestra began to play, and Newton sang—his voice warbling.

"What do you see when you look at me?
A monster, a creature, a beast?
When you see me, why do you flee?
Give me a chance, please, at least."

Newton finished.

"Did somebody let loose a frog in here?" Mimi asked, and a few kids tittered.

"There certainly was an amphibious quality to your singing, Newton," Professor Snollygoster said. "But a good job with the emotion! You may leave the stage."

Relieved, Newton walked off.

"Did I really sound like a frog?" he asked as he squeezed between Theremin and Shelly.

"Maybe a little," Shelly admitted. "But don't worry. The singing is the hardest part. Just wait until you hear everybody else."

"And now we'll hear auditions for the role of Igor, Dr. Frankenstein's assistant," Snollygoster continued. "Once again there is only one student auditioning for this role: Rotwang."

The tall teen shuffled up onto the stage and pushed a strand of greasy hair away from his eyes.

"All right, then, Rotwang. Sing the song, please," Snollygoster said. "And remember, let's hear some emotion!"

The robot orchestra played, and Rotwang began to do something that resembled singing but was actually just a mumbling monotone.

> *"My name is Igor.*
> *I'll do any chore.*
> *I don't need to think.*
> *I skulk and I slink."*

"Oh dear," Snollygoster said. "Rotwang, that was entirely devoid of emotion. We need to understand Igor's feelings."

Rotwang shrugged. "Whatever you say."

Snollygoster sighed and looked at his tablet. "Is there nobody else who wants to try out for the assistant?"

The auditorium was so quiet, you could have heard an amoeba burp.

"Nobody wants to play the role of the assistant," Shelly whispered to Newton. "It would be an insult to their mad-scientist families."

"Well, I don't care what part I get, as long as I get

a part," Newton said. "Maybe I should try out for the assistant?"

"Snollygoster said he might put people in different parts than they tried out for," Shelly replied. "I hope you get something good!"

"All right, then, let us begin the auditions for the role of Dr. Frankenstein," Snollygoster said. "First up is Higglesworth Vollington."

Pffft. pffft. pffft. Higgy made farting noises as he walked up the stairs and onto the stage—not on purpose, but because he had stuffed his feet-shaped green goo into rubber boots. Instead of his usual heavy coat, he wore a lab coat like Dr. Frankenstein would have, but he still wore rubber gloves on his hands and a knit cap on his head. As usual, his eyes peeked out from behind thick goggles, but the rest of his face was bandaged.

"Er, Higgy, are you sure you don't want to try out for the Monster?" Snollygoster asked.

"Sir, I am insulted," Higgy replied in his British accent. "For one thing, Dr. Frankenstein was from England, and only *I* have the voice for the part. For another, did you not yourself say that appearance did not matter in the casting of the musical? Let me audition, and you will see that I have the spirit of the great doctor!"

"Very well," Snollygoster replied.

Higgy began. "Theycallmeamadscientist," he said, reciting the first line of the Dr. Frankenstein monologue at a really fast pace. He finished the monologue in record time, and then began to sing.

"I am Doctor Frankenstein.
I can't do anything to help you
If you've got a bad flu,
But if you're looking for something new,
Then I'm the doctor for you!"

Everyone stared at Higgy, stunned. He had an amazing voice! Then . . .

Pffft! Pffft! Pffft!

Three involuntary squishy fart noises erupted from Higgy's feet as he shuffled his legs.

Professor Snollygoster coughed. "That certainly shows . . . spirit, Higgy," he said. "Mimi Crowninshield, you are next!"

Before she climbed onto the stage, Mimi handed the professor a white rose.

"I just wanted to thank you for directing the musical, Professor," she said sweetly. "And I want you to know that I don't want any special consideration for the role of Dr. Frankenstein, even though my parents' company is donating money to build the set. I want to get this part purely based on my talent."

Snollygoster sniffed the flower. "Don't try to fool an emotional chemistry professor with chemistry," he said. "I can smell Metzger's Mind Control Formula from a mile away, Mimi. It appears that perhaps you are not so confident in your talent if you have to resort to a trick like this?"

Mimi turned bright red. "But I am confident. I am!" she said, snatching the rose and stomping onto the stage.

"She should be disqualified!" Theremin called out.

"On the contrary, such careful planning shows that Mimi does indeed have the spirit of the great doctor," Snollygoster said. "Let's see what you've got, Mimi."

Mimi sang the song in a loud, clear voice—without making any farting noises.

She's not bad, Newton thought, and he glanced at Shelly. She was biting her lower lip, and Newton guessed that Mimi's performance had her a little worried.

"Excellent, Mimi," Professor Snollygoster said. "Now let's hear some lines from the monologue."

Mimi cleared her throat. "They call me a mad scientist," she said. "But if I am mad, then so is wanting to help humanity. If I am mad, so is wanting to explore new frontiers. If I am mad, so is wanting to test the limits of my genius to see what I can do. If these things make me mad, then call me mad! *Mwah, ha, ha, ha, ha.*"

Mimi sounded impressive, but Newton noticed that she didn't move around the stage at all when she talked. She looked a little stiff.

"Thank you, Mimi," Snollygoster said. "Next, Shelly Ravenholt."

Shelly stood up and took a deep breath.

"You'll do great, Shelly!" Newton said as she squeezed past him.

"You can do it, Shelly!" Theremin encouraged her.

Shelly got up onstage and sang the song. Newton thought she sounded great. Then Snollygoster asked her to perform the monologue.

Shelly took another deep breath. She turned and walked away from the audience. Newton turned to Theremin. What was she doing?

She began to pace the stage like a person with a flame burning inside them. "They call me a mad scientist," she began. "But if I am mad, then so is wanting to help humanity. If I am mad, so is wanting to explore new frontiers. If I am mad, so is wanting to test the limits of my genius to see what I can do."

Everyone gazed at Shelly in awe. Newton finally knew what Snollygoster meant about speaking the lines with emotion. Just watching her, he felt excited, electrified.

Shelly's eyes blazed as she delivered the last line. "If

these things make me mad, then CALL ME MAD!" She then released an evil cackle that gave Newton chills up and down his spine.

Some kids started applauding. A rare smile spread on Snollygoster's face.

"Magnificent, Shelly!" he said, and Mimi scowled. "Now let us hear from the rest of you auditioning for Dr. Frankenstein—all twenty-seven of you."

One by one, the rest of the mad-scientist hopefuls took the stage. Odifin Pinkwad sang in a monotone voice and read a different monologue that he had written himself. "For what is a mad scientist except a brain? A big, wonderful, all-powerful brain?"

Snollygoster did not seem impressed.

Some kids had good voices. Some kids had good mad-scientist laughs. But nobody channeled Dr. Frankenstein the way Shelly had.

"Shelly, you've got this in the bag," Theremin told her.

When the last student vying for the Dr. Frankenstein part had auditioned, Professor Snollygoster consulted his tablet. "Let's see," he said. "We have only two auditioners left. Tori Twitcher, you asked if you could play the castle cat. There is no cat in this musical, but I will see if I can work it into the script. No audition necessary."

"Thank you so meow," Tori replied.

"And finally, there is Theremin Rozika," Professor Snollygoster said. "Theremin, I see here that you want to play the Castle Cook? But that role has only one line."

Theremin stood up. "That's right," he said. "I have it memorized. 'Does this need more salt?'"

"That is very good, Theremin, but I have seen your emotions on full display, and they are quite marvelous," Snollygoster said. "I'd love to see you try out for a bigger role. Perhaps Igor?"

Theremin's eyes flashed red. "Why Igor? Why not the doctor? Is it because I'm a robot, and we're supposed to serve humans?"

"Not at all," Snollygoster said. "The role of Igor is a very complex one. He is conflicted. He wants to serve his master, but he fears that what he is doing is wrong. I need a great actor for this role, and I think you could be a great actor."

"I just want a small part," Theremin insisted. "I've got a big test to study for."

"I really wish you'd reconsider it," Snollygoster said. "I believe you have the soul of an Igor, Theremin. You'd be wonderful."

"Hey, what about Rotwang?" Odifin piped up, but Snollygoster ignored him. Rotwang just shrugged, not looking too disappointed.

"The *soul* of Igor?" Theremin replied. "So you *do* think I'm inferior to humans. I knew it!" Sparks began to fly from his joints, and Newton could feel heat radiating from the metal.

"It takes a great actor to play an unlikable character, Theremin," Snollygoster countered. "I am giving you a high compliment. I understand that you have a test to study for, but acting is a challenge worth taking on. Acting will teach you things. It's like life. You never know what you will feel, learn, or discover about yourself."

That made sense to Newton, and it made him even more eager to get a part in the musical. But Theremin was literally steaming with anger.

"I said, NOOOOOO!" Theremin's eyes flashed red, and he stormed out of the auditorium. Newton and Shelly hurried after him, and Higgy followed.

"DID YOU HEAR HIM?" Theremin fumed. "HE THINKS I'M INFERIOR!"

"That's not what he said," Newton told him. "He said—"

"DON'T TELL ME WHAT HE SAID," Theremin shouted. "I KNOW WHAT I HEARD."

Shelly touched Theremin's arm, and then pulled her hand away. "Ow, you're burning up!" she said. "Come on, Theremin, let's go cool down."

Theremin's eyes flickered, still bright with anger.

Newton knew that if anybody could calm him down, it was Shelly.

"Where are we going?" Higgy asked as Shelly raced down the hallway.

"The Smart Scoop," Shelly answered.

Outside the school, in the tropical jungle, a few shops and restaurants catered to the needs of the students and staff. The Smart Scoop was an ice cream parlor that had recently opened.

When they reached the shop, a sign informed them:

TREATS DESIGNED FOR YOUR DNA!

GIVE US A SAMPLE, WE'LL GIVE YOU A PERSONALIZED SUNDAE!

Inside, a young man wearing glasses and a nametag that read SPENCER looked up from the register and held up a pair of scissors. "Welcome to the Smart Scoop. May I please have a hair sample?"

"Not right now," Shelly said. "May we use your freezer, please?"

Spencer saw the smoke coming out of Theremin's ears and nodded. Shelly ushered him to the walk-in freezer and shut the door.

"Let's just give him a minute," she said.

"Want a sundae while you wait?" Spencer asked.

"Sure," Newton said. "How does it work?"

Spencer held up the scissors. "We take a strand of your hair and run a DNA analysis. Then we make you an ice cream sundae with ingredients that are optimal for your body type, most likely taste preferences, and more."

"I'll try," Shelly offered.

Spencer snipped off a strand of her hair and fed it into a large machine behind him. Buttons beeped and flashed different colors. Then a door opened, and an ice-cream sundae slid out on a conveyor belt as a short explanation popped up on a screen. He handed the sundae to Shelly and read the text. "Let's see. It says, 'Coconut milk gelato, because you most likely have some trouble digesting cow's milk, sprinkled with dark chocolate shavings to boost your endorphins because, well, why not?'"

"Yummy!" Shelly said.

"You're lucky. You wouldn't believe some of the sundaes I've had to serve, and we just opened. Who's next?"

"I'll give it a try," Newton offered.

Spencer snipped a hair from Newton's head and fed it into the machine. Moments later a sundae came out. "Hmm. All it says is, 'Vanilla ice cream with candied crickets,' but it doesn't say why. I wonder if the machine is working?" he wondered aloud.

"It's okay. I'll taste it," Newton said, and Spencer handed it to him with a shrug.

Newton dipped his spoon into one of the scoops and took the tiniest taste. To his surprise, he didn't just like it, he loved it. "Wow, it's perfect."

"Can I try?" Higgy asked, always willing to eat anything. Newton motioned for him to go ahead, so he grabbed a clean spoon and dug in. "Mmm, delightfully crunchy with a nice fleck of vanilla bean flavor. Not bad!" Then he let out a massive burp, in his ultimate seal of approval.

Spencer eyed Higgy. "And what about your . . . friend?"

"The name's Higgy," he said. "And I don't have any hair. Would a drop of goo do?"

Spencer shrugged. "I guess we can try it."

Higgy took off his hat, revealing green protoplasm. Spencer gently used the tip of the scissors to remove a drop of goo. Then he put it into the machine.

The machine beeped and buzzed. The door slid open, and out came . . . a cup of lime gelatin.

"Excellent. My favorite!" Higgy cried.

"I didn't even know the machine could make gelatin," Spencer said. "But here you go. It says, 'Lime gelatin with a surprise inside, because you look like lime gelatin and pranks are in your DNA.'"

Higgy took a bite, and as he ate the lime gelatin it turned his gooey body from green to purple! Another message

popped onto the screen and Spencer read it aloud. "It says, 'Don't worry. It is only temporary. Gotcha!'"

Higgy started laughing and everyone joined in. He, Newton, and Shelly had just sat down at a table when Theremin emerged from the freezer, looking cool and calm . . . until he saw Higgy, and looked confused by his purple color. A few seconds later Higgy was back to his usual gooey green self again.

"Better now?" Shelly asked Theremin.

"I think so," Theremin said. "Sorry about that. We should be celebrating Shelly's amazing audition, not worrying about me."

"We *all* did great," Shelly said.

"I know I was nervous about it, but now I'm kind of excited," Newton remarked. "I hope I get a part."

"That reminds me," Shelly said. "Newton, we need to talk about what happened when you got nervous. You camouflaged!"

"He did?" Higgy asked.

"He did, and it's a good thing we were in the back, and nobody saw us," Shelly went on. "Newton, if you can't control your strange powers, everyone is going to know your secret!"

It was a problem that even his vanilla-cricket ice-cream sundae couldn't solve.

CHAPTER 4

Surprise!

Newton stopped crunching on crickets and froze. Shelly was right. Camouflaging in the auditorium had been a close call—too close.

"Hold on, now," Higgy said. "Why does Newton need to conceal his special abilities? He's certainly not the only student here who is . . . more than human, let's say. Myself being example one. And then, of course, there's Odifin, and Theremin, and—"

"I'm not the only robot in school either," Theremin pointed out.

"Yeah, maybe I should just, you know, not worry about it," Newton said.

Shelly frowned. "I don't know, Newton. This whole thing with Flubitus has got me spooked. I trust Mumtaz, but I can't shake the feeling that there's something really weird happening. And if your abilities are part of that, maybe we need to find out more about them before *everybody* knows."

"I think Shelly has a point," Theremin said. "Maybe it is best to keep your specialness under wraps for a little while longer."

Higgy sighed. "I live my life here under wraps." He motioned to his bandaged face. "I wish I could just be free to be me, even though most people can't handle it. But it's up to you, Newton."

Newton thought for a moment. He agreed with Shelly that it seemed something weird was happening—something weirder than Mumtaz would admit. Plus, there was another reason why he liked the idea.

"Okay," Newton said. "I kind of like blending in, anyway."

"At least you *can* blend in," Higgy said, before noisily slurping down a spoonful of lime gelatin and turning an even darker shade of purple.

"I'm just worried that next time you're going to freak out about something and camouflage in plain sight where everyone can see you," Shelly said. "Are you sure you can't control it?"

Newton shrugged. "I'm not sure. It just kind of . . . happens."

Shelly's eyes twinkled with excitement. "I know. Let's

run tests on your camouflage abilities! You can work on trying to control them."

"You guys have fun," Theremin said. "I have that big programming test to study for."

"Oh, come on, Theremin, we need you," Shelly coaxed.

"Do you really?" he asked. "Or do you just need Newton? Everything's always about Newton, isn't it? *He's* the one with the special abilities. *He's* the one who's going to save the school."

"Okay, okay, you're overheating again," Shelly said. "Do you need to go back into the freezer?"

"It will be a lot more fun with you," Newton said.

"What about me? I'm fun!" Higgy said.

"You are," Newton agreed. "And you know, it's better when we all do things together. The four of us."

Theremin sighed. "Fine. If I have time, I'll help. When did you want to do this?"

"We need a few days to come up with a plan," Shelly answered. She checked her schedule on her tablet. "How about Saturday morning?"

Before anyone could answer, a strange noise came from under the table.

"Abbblrdrrrrpp!"

"Higgy, was that you?" Theremin asked.

"Nope," Higgy replied.

Shelly knew that sound. She looked under the table. "It's Peewee!" she cried. She reached down and came up holding the furry blue creature. "How did you get out of the rescue lab?"

"Abbblrdrrrrpp!"

Peewee scurried up Shelly's arm and rubbed his furry head on her neck.

"Aww, you are so cute!" Shelly said. "But you can't be with me all the time, Peewee."

"Why can't he?" Newton asked. "I think he's going to come after you every time you leave him behind, anyway."

"You have a point," Shelly said. "But first things first, Newton. I'm going to make a plan to help us figure out if there's any way to control your camouflaging. Don't worry. We're going to figure it out."

I sure hope so! Newton thought.

Ca-wee! Ca-wee! Ca-wee!

The sound of one of Shelly's monsters woke Newton up at six o'clock on Saturday morning.

"What is it, Woller?" Newton asked, yawning. He brushed away the wings that the fuzzy purple creature was flapping near his face. Woller dropped a rolled-up

piece of paper onto Newton's chest and then flew away.

Newton unrolled the note.

Eat breakfast. Then head to the pool to start camouflage testing. —Shelly

"Shelly's taking this a little too seriously, Higgy," Newton muttered, and he hopped off his bunk. But Higgy wasn't in the bottom bunk. "Higgy?" *I guess he already left,* Newton thought.

He quickly got dressed, used the bathroom, and headed to the school cafeteria for breakfast. Since it was so early on a Saturday morning, most kids were still asleep. He sucked down a smoothie and then headed to the pool, which was inside the gym.

It was eerily quiet when Newton entered the gym. Normally, there'd be a kid lifting weights in the antigravity chamber, but it was empty. (The weights weren't heavy at all once gravity was removed, so it was a real confidence-booster.) There was nobody playing laser tennis or practicing extra-hot yoga in the lava pits.

When he reached the pool room, it was deserted too. The robot lifeguards were powered off and charging up next to a NO SWIMMING sign. The lights in the room were off, but the levitation projectors that suspended the pool above the gym floor were on. The water rippled in the dim light.

"Hello?" Newton called out. "Shelly?"

Then he heard a strange, bubbling sound behind him. He turned to see an enormous creature emerge from the water! It looked like a . . . His mind searched for the word. A sea serpent? With black scales, yellow eyes, and fins on either side of its head.

The creature leaned toward Newton and roared, revealing a mouth of sharp fangs.

"Roooowwwwwwr!"

"*Aaaaaaaaaaaaah!*" Newton screeched.

Then the monster suddenly vanished, and Newton heard Shelly's voice.

"Interesting," she said. "You went from Newton to camouflage in three point eight-nine seconds."

Newton looked down at himself—and saw that his entire body, including his clothes, matched the floor below him and the wall behind him.

"Can you snap out of it?" Shelly asked, looking slightly at the wrong spot since she couldn't see him.

"I think so," Newton said, and he concentrated. Slowly his normal coloration returned.

"So this was a trick?" he asked.

"No, an experiment," Shelly explained. "You camouflage yourself when you're frightened, and it's much easier to frighten someone who's not expecting it."

"Oh," Newton said. "That makes sense. Should I be on the lookout for more surprises?"

"No, not today," Shelly said. "The whole idea is to surprise you, right?"

"Right. So, did you learn anything?" Newton asked.

"Well, it's good to know how many seconds it takes for the camouflage to kick in," she replied. "Because if you're going to want to control it, you only have a short time to act."

"And where did that monster come from?" Newton asked.

Shelly grinned and held up a tiny remote control. "It's a hologram," she said. "Tootie helped me program it."

"Nice," Newton admitted. He yawned. "Why did we have to get up so early for this?"

"I wanted to use the pool, and it opens at seven," she replied. "I thought the pool would be a good start, because this is the first place I saw you camouflage. Remember?"

"Yeah. The first time you showed me the pool, I jumped right in, with all my clothes on," he replied. "I couldn't help myself."

"But see, you're not doing that now," Shelly pointed out. "So you can control your instincts to some extent, right?"

"I guess," Newton said. "So what now?"

"I'm going back to my dorm to work on something for Peewee," she replied. "You can help, if you want."

"Sure," Newton answered.

They headed out of the gym and down the hallway. Suddenly Shelly tripped. The remote control flew out of her hand and skidded under the door to the boys' bathroom.

"Newton, would you mind getting that for me?" she asked.

"No problem," Newton said. He entered the bathroom and looked on the floor for the remote.

BAM!

One of the bathroom stall doors burst open. A creature with glowing eyes and a pumpkin for a head came out of the stall, a pitchfork in its hand.

"Aaaaaaaah!" Newton screamed, flattening himself against the bathroom wall.

The pumpkin creature started to laugh. Newton knew that laugh, and slowly realized the pumpkin creature had a familiar-looking metal body that looked a lot like that of a certain robot he knew.

"Theremin?" he asked.

Theremin took the plastic pumpkin off his head. "It's me. Hey, good job camouflaging!"

Newton looked down at himself and saw a pattern of flasks, atoms, Tesla coils, and bolts of lightning all over his body. Looking behind him, he saw that he matched the wallpaper!

Shelly peeked her head around the door to see the action.

Theremin announced, "Two point nine-six seconds. Impressive, considering the complicated pattern you re-created."

"I thought you said you weren't going to scare me

anymore!" Newton said as his coloring returned.

Shelly grinned. "If I had told you, you wouldn't have been surprised," she said. "But don't worry. That was the last test for today."

The three friends left the bathroom and walked outside into the jungle.

"I hope I didn't frighten you too badly, Newton," Theremin said.

"It's okay," Newton replied. "I mean, I think if I had seen you with the pumpkin head just walking down the hall, I wouldn't have been scared. It was the shock that did it."

"That's going to be a challenge," Shelly said. "Helping you figure out how to control the impulse when something unexpected happens."

Their feet crunched along the path as they walked past the leafy green trees and brightly colored flowers of the island. Birds swooped overhead and called to one another with loud squawks and chirps.

Newton felt something tickle his foot. He looked down to see an enormous, green snake beginning to twist around his ankle.

"Very funny, guys," he said. "Is this a robot snake? Or is it Higgy? I bet it's Higgy. Higgy, did you squeeze into a snake costume?"

Shelly's eyes got wide. "Newton, don't move! That's a python! It could squeeze you to death!"

"Right," Newton said with sarcasm in his voice. "Just like that sea serpent was going to eat me. But I don't believe it. It's doesn't even look—*blllrrrrrrrp!*"

The snake wrapped itself tightly around Newton's waist, making it hard for him to breathe. Newton's vision started to blur. Through the haze, he saw Higgy walking down the path toward him.

"Sorry I'm late," Higgy said. "Where's Newton?"

It had just clicked in Newton's head that the snake was real!

Somebody do something! Newton silently screamed.

Bzzzzzt! Theremin shot laser beams from his eyes and zapped the snake, being extra careful not to hit Newton. Startled, the snake let go of its grasp on Newton and slithered away. Shelly ran toward him.

"Newton, are you all right? Can you breathe?"

Newton took a deep breath. "Yeah, I'm okay. You didn't set that up, did you?"

Shelly shook her head. "No, but it was still a valid test. It took you four point seven-three seconds to camouflage this time. But the results were spectacular."

She showed him a picture on her phone. The

camouflage job was so good that it was hard to make out Newton, but then he spotted the outline of his body. He had sprouted a pattern of green leaves and flowers to match the jungle.

"We need to figure out what all this data means," Shelly said.

"Fine," Newton agreed. "But can we do it in your dorm room? Away from . . . here?"

The four friends went to Shelly's room.

"I'm disappointed I didn't get a chance to scare you, Newton," Higgy said. "I got up early and everything, but then I saw the pudding delivery pod touch down outside the cafeteria, and, well . . . I got a little carried away." He burped to emphasize his point.

"That's fine. I got scared just fine without you," Newton said with a sigh.

"So now we know that you can camouflage when you're afraid, and we have an idea of how long it takes for the ability to kick in," Shelly said. "What we don't know is if you can control it."

"You mean, stop myself before it happens?" Newton asked.

Shelly nodded. "Yes. And also, if you can camouflage on purpose. Can you try it now?" She pointed to her wall, where she had posters of famous scientists.

Newton shrugged. "Sure, I'll give it a try."

He stood in front of the wall and closed his eyes.

Camouflage, he coached himself. *Blend in with the wall.*

He opened an eye. "Is anything happening?"

"Not yet," Theremin reported.

Newton turned to the wall. Next to him was a poster of a woman with gray hair in a bun on her head, wearing an old-fashioned dress. The name on the poster read MARIE CURIE.

Newton closed his eyes again, thinking of the poster. Suddenly he heard Shelly gasp.

"Newton, take a few steps forward," she said.

Newton opened his eyes and obeyed. His friends were staring at him, wide-eyed.

"What's happening?" Newton asked.

"Go to the mirror," Shelly told him.

He did, and the reflection he saw was the woman in the poster. It wasn't a pattern printed on him—it *was* him. His face was her face. He wore the same dress as in the poster. He didn't feel any different—but he looked like a different person.

"This is amazing, Newton!" Shelly said. "You're not just camouflaging—you're mimicking! It's a more sophisticated ability. It reminds me of *Thaumoctopus*

mimicus, an octopus that can change its coloration and the shape of its body to look like a predator."

"Am I going to get stuck like this?" Newton asked nervously.

"Close your eyes now and imagine looking like

yourself again," Theremin suggested.

Newton did it, and when he opened his eyes, he saw his own reflection. He sighed with relief.

"Can we try it with another subject?" Shelly asked. "Maybe Theremin."

"Sure," Newton replied. He stared at Theremin for a minute, and then he closed his eyes.

After a minute he heard Theremin shout, "No way!" He opened his eyes and looked in the mirror.

He looked just like Theremin! It was exciting and terrifying at the same time.

"Wow," he said.

"You look like twins!" Higgy remarked. "Well done, Newton."

"I can't stay like this. It's weird," Newton said, and he closed his eyes and reverted back to normal.

"I'm really excited about this," Shelly said. "Can you imagine how useful this ability could be?"

"I don't know," Newton said. "I think I'd rather just be myself."

"I get it. And we still need to figure out how to help you control the camouflaging," Shelly continued.

"I can teach Newton some calming techniques," Theremin offered.

Shelly, Newton, and Higgy stared at Theremin as if

he had suddenly grown a third metal arm and eaten a sandwich.

"Um, no offense, but when have you ever been calm? We literally had to stick you in a freezer the other day," Shelly pointed out.

"Mumtaz taught me some techniques the last time I was in detention for throwing a tantrum in class," Theremin replied. "Just because I don't *use* them doesn't mean I don't know about them."

"Okay, great," Newton said. "What did you learn?"

"Well, the first thing you can do when you get scared and don't want to camouflage is try to count to ten—" Theremin said.

Shelly interrupted. "I don't think that will work. He camouflages in less than ten seconds."

Theremin's eyes flashed. "Okay. Then how about visualizing something calm? Like a sunset or a cute kitten?"

"I could try that," Newton said.

"How is Newton supposed to conjure up a calm image when his fight-or-flight response is kicking in?" Shelly asked. "That doesn't seem practical."

"FINE," Theremin said loudly. "I've never tried this one, since I can't really breathe, but taking deep breaths is supposed to help."

Shelly frowned. "Maybe, but—"

Theremin pretended to breathe in deeply, then breathe out again, but before he could begin another breath, he lost his temper. "SHELLY, HOW DO YOU EXPECT ME TO TEACH NEWTON HOW TO BE CALM IF YOU KEEP SHOOTING DOWN ALL MY IDEAS?" Theremin yelled.

"See what I mean?" Shelly said.

"I think the deep breaths sound good," Newton said. "Maybe I can try that the next time you decide to scare me. We could schedule—"

"BOO!" Higgy's eyes popped out of his face on long goo stalks, and stopped just in front of Newton's eyeballs. Newton didn't even remember to think about taking deep breaths. He automatically camouflaged to blend in to Shelly's bedspread.

"See? No time," Shelly said.

"Whatever," Theremin said glumly. "I'm going to study." He left the room, slamming the door behind him.

"How was that scare, Shelly?" Higgy asked.

"Spectacular, Higgy," Shelly replied.

"Yeah, really good," Newton said, but he was anxious.

If I can't control my abilities, pretty soon everyone will know my secret, he thought. *How long will it be before everyone knows how different I am from everybody else?*

CHAPTER 5

Does This Need More Salt?

On Monday morning Ms. Mumtaz's hologram appeared in the cafeteria again.

"Students, Professor Snollygoster has chosen the actors for the roles in the musical," she began. "He asked me to remind you that if you didn't get the part you wanted, please try to keep your emotions under control. He did what was best for the production."

A murmur went up among the students. Newton felt an unfamiliar thrill course through him. This was exciting!

It would be nice to play the Monster, he thought. *But I don't care what part I get. I just want to be in the play!*

"So without further ado . . . ," Ms. Mumtaz said, and her face disappeared and was replaced by an image of a castle with a thunderstorm brewing overhead.

A deep voice began to speak. "In a time when humans feared science and logic, one person was not afraid to experiment. To explore. To learn. And that person was . . .

Dr. Frankenstein!" The lightning flashed, and the castle was replaced by a shadowy figure in a lab coat.

The deep voice spoke again. "Franken-Sci High will honor this great genius with *Frankenstein: The Musical*, an extravaganza of song, dance, and special effects!"

"We know that already!" Boris Bacon shouted. "Tell us who got the parts!"

Lightning flashed in the hologram again.

"Frankenstein: The Musical," the voice intoned. "Starring . . . Shelly Ravenholt as Dr. Frankenstein!"

Shelly gasped as her face appeared as a hologram in the middle of the cafeteria. Theremin let out a cheer.

Newton hugged her. "You did it, Shelly!"

The announcer continued. "Higglesworth Vollington as the Monster!"

If it's not me, at least it's Higgy, Newton thought. He turned to high-five his friend, but Higgy was looking down at the floor.

The faces of the students cast in the play appeared one by one as the announcer called them out.

"Rotwang as Igor! Odifin Pinkwad as Dr. Henry Clerval! Tootie Van der Flootin as Sea Captain Walton! Gustav Goddard as the Best Friend! Theremin Rozika as the Castle Cook! Tori Twitcher as the Castle Cat! Mimi Crowninshield as the Lead Angry Villager!

SHELLY RAVENHOLT

And Boris Bacon, Debbie Darwin, Faraday Michaels, Minerva Kepler, Archimedes Jones, and Newton Warp as our Chorus of Angry Villagers."

Newton grinned when he saw his face appear with the rest of the Angry Villagers. That was him! He'd made it! And better yet—he was part of something. That felt really good.

The faces of the cast disappeared, and Ms. Mumtaz appeared again.

"Congratulations, cast," she said. "The first rehearsal will be held today in the school auditorium, right after the last class."

Her hologram vanished, and the cafeteria erupted with noise as everyone began talking about the casting. Several kids came up to congratulate Shelly. But Mimi stomped up, her face red with anger.

"This is totally unfair, Shelly!" she said. "You only got the role because of your family connections, and you know it."

Shelly stood up. "That is not true, Mimi," she said. "My parents don't even know I tried out for the role."

Mimi folded her arms across her chest. "Likely story," she said. "I will not stand for this! I will march on Ms. Mumtaz's office! I will storm Snollygoster's lab! I will—"

"Sounds like you're practicing for your role of

Lead Angry Villager, Mimi," Theremin said.

Mimi spun around. "At least I've got more lines than you. The Castle Cook? What kind of a role is that?"

Theremin's eyes flashed red, but he tried to hide his anger with his reply. "As a matter of fact, it's the role I wanted."

"That figures," Mimi said. "Always letting your friend Shelly get the spotlight, right?"

Newton spoke up. "Leave Shelly alone, Mimi," he said. "You're always talking about your family, and how you should get special treatment at the school because they're so rich and powerful and stuff."

"That's right," Shelly said. "Don't you get a dorm room all to yourself, with the best view? And aren't professors excusing you for being late all the time, just because you're a Crowninshield?"

"That's different!" Mimi shot back.

"How?" Newton asked.

"It—It doesn't matter," she said. She stepped closer to Shelly's face. "Just you wait. I will—ow!"

Peewee had come out of nowhere, run across the table, and jumped up to bop Mimi on the nose. Then the creature scurried up Shelly's arm.

Mimi scowled, covering her nose with her hand. "That does it! I'll get you, Shelly Ravenholt, and your little . . . blue furry thing, too!"

Mimi stormed off.

"Don't let Mimi spoil your good news, Shelly," Newton said. "It's awesome that you got the part that you wanted."

"At least somebody did," Higgy mumbled.

"I'm sorry, Higgy," Shelly said. "I know you wanted to play the doctor."

"I'd be happy with any human role," he said. "Being cast as the Monster . . . it's insulting. They should have given the role to Newton. At least he wanted it."

"But I can't sing," Newton pointed out. "And you have an amazing voice. I bet that's why Snollygoster gave you the role."

"*Hmpppppf!*" Higgy said, and he squished away without another word.

"Poor Higgy," Shelly said, and sighed. "I can't believe our first rehearsal is today. We're going to be so busy! And I still need to find a way to keep Peewee from escaping all the time."

She scratched Peewee's head. "No bopping, Peewee. Not even Mimi. Okay?"

"*Abbblrdrrrrpp!*"

Then she sighed. "What if Mimi's right? I mean, what if Snollygoster gave me the role because I'm related to the Frankensteins, and not because I'm good at acting?"

"But you *were* good," Newton said.

"The best," Theremin added. "And everyone will see that at today's rehearsal!"

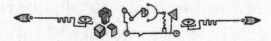

When Newton, Theremin, Shelly, and Higgy arrived at the auditorium after school, Mimi was yelling at Professor Snollygoster.

"It's not fair!" she fumed. "My parents are launching into an investigation of this, and when they're done, you won't be directing this musical anymore. I will! I will star and direct! I will!"

"Miss Crowninshield, I must ask you to calm down," Snollygoster said.

"Make me!" Mimi responded, egging him on.

"Very well." The professor took a small bottle from his pocket and opened it. A curlicue of liquid made its way from the bottle to Mimi's face. Immediately she quieted down.

"I will—what was I saying?" Mimi asked.

"You were just telling me that you were about to sit down so we could proceed with the rehearsal," Snollygoster said.

Newton whispered to Theremin. "What was that?"

Theremin used his enhanced telescopic vision to read

the label on the bottle. "Calming formula," Theremin replied. "Snollygoster tried to use it on me once, but I don't respond to chemistry."

"Now then," Snollygoster said loudly, and he pointed to a circle of chairs set up on the stage. "I'd like everyone to take a seat and find the scripts I sent to all your tablets. Today we're going to begin with a read-through of the speaking parts. We'll have separate rehearsals for the musical numbers later on."

"What if we don't have a speaking part?" asked Minerva, one of the other kids besides Newton playing an Angry Villager.

"The Angry Villagers will have plenty of yelling and rabble-rousing to contribute," Snollygoster promised.

"Woo-hoo!" cheered Boris.

"Please take your seats," Snollygoster said.

"I need to say something first," Higgy spoke up.

Snollygoster sighed. "What is it, Higgy? We need to get this rehearsal started."

"It was totally unfair of you to cast me as the Monster," Higgy said. "I told you that I wanted a human role. Everyone at school already thinks that I'm a monster. I wanted to show my human side."

"That's exactly why I cast you as the Monster," Snollygoster said. "You are an excellent actor, and you

will show the audience that the Monster is a being with feelings and intelligence, and not just a hideous beast."

Boris piped up. "Also, Higgy can do cool things, like change shape and make his eyeballs pop out of his head."

"That, too," Snollygoster admitted.

"Hey, if Higgy doesn't want to play the Monster, why don't we just make one?" Tootie asked. "The Monster Club could create something."

"After the Peewee incident, the school has become stricter about monster creations," Snollygoster replied. "Besides, Higgy really is a wonderful actor. The play wouldn't be the same without him."

Professor Snollygoster turned to Higgy. "Is there any way I can convince you to take this part?"

Behind his bandages, Higgy's protoplasm bubbled like simmering soup as he thought. Finally he answered. "Maybe if there is a human role I could play too," he suggested. "Even a small part. Just so I can show that I can do more than be monstrous."

Snollygoster brightened. "That's an excellent solution! I will come up with a human role just for you, Higgy. Do we have a deal?"

Higgy held out a gloved hand. "Deal," he said.

They shook on it, making a squishy sound.

"Fine, then," Snollygoster said. "Now I must insist that we start this rehearsal!"

The tone in his voice sent everyone scurrying into the seats onstage and taking out their tablets.

"Captain Walton, please begin," he said.

Tootie cleared her throat. "I'll never forget the day I found the doctor, floating in the middle of the ocean on a small boat. I invited her onto my ship, and asked to hear her story. She told me her name was Dr. Frankenstein . . . and the story she told me is one I shall never forget."

Newton listened, fascinated, as the words on his tablet came alive in the voices of the actors. The musical told the tale of how Dr. Frankenstein shocked the scientific community by creating a monster. Other scientists criticized her, and her best friend abandoned her. When her monster came to life, everyone in the village was afraid of it. They stormed the castle and drove Dr. Frankenstein and the Monster away.

It was amazing! Even though they were just reading the script, and not moving around the stage, Shelly's reading was intense, Higgy's was mesmerizing, Gustav made everyone laugh, and Theremin delivered his one line with pizazz.

"Does this need more salt?" he asked, providing some comic relief by piping in during a tense moment.

When it came time for the Angry Villagers to get angry, Newton yelled and growled and shook his fist in the air. It was exhilarating, because anger wasn't an emotion he usually felt. When the rehearsal ended, he was hoarse but happy.

"Tomorrow we will begin with staging," Snollygoster announced. "And this weekend we will begin musical rehearsals for the solo performers. I want all lines memorized by next week, so get to work right away!"

"That was awesome," Newton remarked as they filed out of the auditorium. He glanced over at Theremin, who looked downcast.

"What's the matter?" Newton asked.

"I wish I had more lines," Theremin admitted. "But I guess it's for the best. I really need to focus on that test. I should head to my room and study."

"Come have dinner with us," Shelly urged. "I mean, I know you're not hungry or anything, but I wanted to talk to you both about something."

Theremin sighed. "Fine. But just for a little while."

Newton put an arm around the robot. "Don't worry, Theremin. We'll do whatever we can to help you pass that test!"

CHAPTER 6

Lizard Boy!

"Does this need more salt?" Theremin asked, putting a plate of French fries in front of Shelly at dinner a little while later.

"I think they are salty enough—oh, I get it. That's your line!" Shelly said.

Newton laughed. "You've got that line down perfect!"

"Well, it's just one line," Theremin said. "I mean, if I couldn't get one line right, it would be pretty sad!"

"And you sounded great, Shelly," Newton said, taking a bite of one of the Mongolian stew balls on his plate.

"Thanks," she said, smiling. "I had a lot of fun doing it. I'm even thinking of finally asking to use my portal pass to do some research for the role. I didn't know where I wanted to go when I first won the pass, but now I think it might help me get into character if I can go home and talk to my parents about our Frankenstein family history and look at original documents and

things. I'm going to ask if I can go tomorrow."

"Your parents aren't upset that you're playing Dr. Frankenstein?" Higgy asked. "What about the Ravenholt-Frankenstein feud?"

"That was a long time ago, and my parents think it was all pretty silly," Shelly replied. "They were thrilled when I called and told them I got the part."

Newton felt a little pang of jealousy. He didn't have anyone to call and tell about his part. Shelly and Theremin and Higgy were all he had.

"But anyway, Newton, what I wanted to say was that even though we'll all be busy rehearsing the musical, I think we should schedule a time to do some more tests on you," Shelly said.

Newton frowned. "I don't think I need any more tests."

"But, Newton, what if you camouflage in front of people? Or someone sees you using your super-sticky fingers?" Shelly asked.

Newton shrugged. "They haven't yet. Well, except Mimi, and she didn't seem to notice when I stuck to the wall of the Airy Café during that glitch in the antigravity system," he said. "And even if they do notice sometime, maybe it won't be a big deal. I mean, Odifin is a brain in a jar. He's not exactly like everyone else."

"And nobody likes him," Theremin pointed out.

"That's because he's *mean*, not because of how he looks," Newton said. "What about Higgy?" He turned to his friend. "You're really different from everybody else, and it's not a big deal, right?"

"Well, to be clear, I'm pretty happy with myself, most of the time. But that's not true of everyone else. Let's see," Higgy said. "I went through seventeen roommates before you agreed to room with me. Nobody likes to eat meals with me—not even you guys, most of the time, even though I know you try to pretend to be cool with how I eat. I'm always last to be picked for the team when we play gravity ball. I—"

"Okay, I get it. It's not easy," Newton said. "But you have a mom and dad, right? A family who loves you?"

"That is true," Higgy replied. "Mummy and Daddy are the best."

"Well, I just don't see how the tests will help me find out who I really am," Newton said. "They make me feel like . . . like a lab animal. And I want to be human."

He saw the hurt look in Higgy's and Theremin's eyes. "I'm not saying it's bad to not be human," Newton said quickly. "It's just . . . I look human, right? So I'd rather just stop the testing and try to, you know, blend in."

"*Blending in* was your problem, mate," Higgy joked.

Shelly looked him in the eyes. "Newton, finding out more about your abilities might help us discover where you came from," she said. "Think about it. You look human, but humans don't have sophisticated defense mechanisms like your camouflage. Humans don't have sticky fingers and toes. You're not like other humans, so we have to ask: Where would other humans like you come from?"

"Also, regular humans don't have bar codes on their feet," Theremin added.

"Okay, I get it! I'm not human!" he said rather loudly.

"Newton, *shhhh*," Shelly warned.

"Why don't you try to get Flubitus to tell you where you came from?" Higgy suggested. "He probably knows."

"Flubitus won't tell me anything. I tried," Newton said. He slammed his fork down on his plate and stood up. "I'll see you guys tomorrow."

"Newton, wait!" Shelly cried.

Newton took the spiral staircase down to the first floor, his heart pounding. He felt angry, and it wasn't a fun kind of angry, like pretending to be a villager. It was a hot, confused anger with sadness mixed in.

I know I'm not human. I know I'm not like everybody else. That's the problem! he thought. *Why doesn't everybody just understand that and leave me alone?*

His friends caught up with him outside on the jungle path.

"Newton, just hear us out," Shelly said. "I still think we can get more information about Flubitus. There's something very strange about his story. I mean, time travel hasn't even been invented yet! So maybe he's lying. But we can't find out unless we talk to him."

"I told you, there's no point," Newton said. "Mumtaz won't tell me anything. Flubitus refused. If we talk to him, I'll just get disappointed again."

"Then let's do more testing," Shelly pressed. "Remember, the camouflage testing unleashed your mimicry ability. Who knows what other superhuman qualities you might have?"

Newton stopped and turned on his heel. "I don't want to be superhuman," he said. "I don't want to do any more testing. I don't want to talk to Flubitus. I JUST WANT TO BE A REGULAR KID! WITH A FAMILY! AND MEMORIES! JUST LIKE EVERYONE ELSE! *Weeeeaaaaaaaa!*"

Newton didn't recognize the noise that came out of his mouth—a loud, squeaky scream. Shelly, Newton, and Higgy were staring at him, wide-eyed. Shelly quickly took a picture of him.

"Newton, are you okay?" she asked.

Theremin looked from side to side. "The coast is clear."

"Why—what did I do?" Newton asked.

Shelly showed him her phone screen. "See for yourself."

Newton stared at the photo. The boy in the picture looked like him, but his skin had turned pale orange, and his fingers were spread wide, and he was jumping in the air. He quickly looked down at himself, and saw that the orange color had faded.

"We need to get to your dorm room," Shelly said.

Newton didn't argue. They hurried to Newton and Higgy's room. Newton and Higgy sat on their bunk beds, and Shelly pushed aside Higgy's mess until she revealed a desk chair and sat down. Theremin hovered by her side.

"So what happened out there?" Newton asked.

"That weird sound you made, and the jumping— that's what geckos do when they get angry," Shelly said. "And chameleons can change color, like you just did. Sometimes they do it when their mood changes. Like when they're frightened."

Newton let this all sink in.

"What does that all mean, then?" he asked.

Higgy piped up. "The evidence points to you being a human-lizard hybrid," he said.

"Lizard Boy! Cool!" Theremin said.

Newton's mind suddenly flashed to the science fair that had happened a few weeks ago. He'd been wearing a pair of Predictive Virtual Reality Goggles, which were supposed to predict the future of any object you focused them on, by allowing you to fast-forward to see what would happen. Newton had focused the goggles on a lizard in a tank and tried to rewind to see the past. He saw the lizard transform from a lizard back into an egg.

Seeing the egg had sparked a memory from deep inside him. He was inside a pod filled with water. There was a bright light around the pod, and he could see shadows. Then the pod cracked open. . . .

Shelly's voice roused him from his flashback. "It may not be as simple as that," she said. "The mimicking ability is an octopus thing."

"Lizard-Octopus Boy!" Theremin cheered.

Newton stared down at his hands as he tried to process this. "But I . . . I don't look like a lizard or an octopus," he said.

"That's what's cool," Shelly said. "Like we've been saying all along, you're a human with special abilities. Superhuman."

I like the sound of that better than "Lizard-Octopus Boy"! Newton thought. *But . . .*

"Do you mean that no other humans can do lizard and octopus stuff?" Newton asked. "Am I the only one?"

"I think so," Shelly answered. "I mean, I've never heard of a human with your abilities. Have you guys?"

Theremin and Higgy shook their heads.

"So how did I get this way?" Newton asked.

"Maybe it's like that superhero Squirrel Girl, who got bit by a flying squirrel, and then got squirrel powers," Theremin suggested.

"So I got bit by a lizard and an octopus?" Newton asked.

"And maybe some other creatures, too," Shelly suggested. "I think we've just scratched the surface of what you can do. If we just do more—"

She stopped herself.

"Testing," Newton finished for her.

"Yeah, testing," Shelly said. "And maybe talk to Flubitus."

"Don't say 'Flubitus'!" Higgy warned. "Newton will freak out!"

Newton blushed. "I won't freak out, I promise."

"Seriously, dude, everyone gets on me for losing my cool, but you need to learn to chill," Theremin said.

"Are you forgetting the time you smashed up the emotional chemistry lab?" Newton asked. "Or smashed through a wall in the nurse's office?"

"That was a door," Theremin corrected him. "And smashing things is something people do when they're angry. Turning orange and making a weird sound . . ."

"I get it," Newton said. "I'm weird."

"Different isn't weird, Newton," Shelly said. "And anyway, knowledge is power. The more you know about yourself, the more power you'll have over your destiny."

Power. Up until now, Newton had felt pretty helpless about what was happening to him. He'd just been going along for the ride.

"Okay," Newton said. "We can do more testing. And talk to Flubitus."

"Let's find him now!" Shelly said eagerly.

"Count me out," Theremin said. "I gotta study."

"I won't do this without Theremin," Newton said. "We're a team. We have to do this together. So tonight, let's help Theremin study instead."

"Whoa, you would do that?" Theremin asked. "Thanks, Newton. But how can you help me study? Do you know computer programming?"

Newton grinned. "I'm superhuman, remember? I'll just use my noodle noggin!"

CHAPTER 7

Croak!

I am inside the pod. I can't see anything through the walls of the pod except for shadowy figures. I hear voices. Suddenly the pod breaks. I spill out, along with the water. The voices gasp. I stand up and see my reflection in a gleaming metal cabinet . . . the face of a green lizard!

Newton woke up in a cold sweat. Sunlight streamed through his dorm room window.

It was just a dream, he thought gratefully.

Then Woller flew up to him.

"Ca-wee! Ca-wee! Ca-wee!"

"I'm awake, Woller. Quiet down!" Newton groaned. Woller dropped a note in front of him and flew away. Newton opened it.

I'm using my portal pass today to go see my parents. I'll be back in time for rehearsal. Can you keep an eye

on Peewee for me? I've programmed robotic food and water dispensers for the other monsters in the rescue lab, but he needs a friend, too. Thank you,
Shelly

"Peewee?" Newton wondered out loud. "Is he in the rescue lab, or—"

"*Ca-wee!*"

Woller flew back into the room, holding Peewee in his claws. He dropped the little monster onto Newton's chest.

"*Abbblrdrrrrpp!*"

"Oh," Newton said. "What exactly am I supposed to do with you, Peewee?"

"*Abbblrdrrrrpp!*"

Higgy plopped out of bed, and his gooey body made a loud squishing sound as he landed on the ground. His eyeballs stared at Newton.

"Am I hearing monster sounds?" he asked.

"Shelly asked me to watch Peewee while she's away today," Newton replied. "But I don't know what to do with him. He always escapes from the rescue lab."

Higgy dug through the stuff piled up on the floor and pulled out a big metal toolbox with a handle that he sometimes used as a lunchbox because it held more

food than a standard-size one. He brought it to his desk and used a tiny laser tool to poke holes in it. Then he brought it to Newton.

"Put Peewee in here," Higgy said.

Newton frowned. "Will he be okay in there?"

"He should be fine," Higgy promised. "You can carry him around with you until Shelly gets back."

Newton jumped down from his bunk and plopped Peewee into the box. Peewee let out one more *"Abbblrdrrrrpp!"* but was quiet after that.

"Thanks, Higgy," Newton said. "You coming to breakfast?"

"Mom sent me a vat of marshmallow-zucchini pudding through the portal post, and I'm going to bring it into the basement to eat it without grossing anyone out," he replied. "But I'll catch up to you later."

"Got it," Newton said.

A short while later he was sucking down a smoothie in the cafeteria with Theremin, taking breaks to carefully drip some of the liquid into the holes in Peewee's container. He could hear the little creature lapping it up inside.

"Thanks for helping me study last night," Theremin said. "Once you switched on your noodle noggin, it was like you were a programming genius."

"Yeah, although I don't remember most of it this morning," Newton admitted. "It's like a brain overload, and only some of it sticks."

Then Newton realized something. "Is that what happens to you, because of the way your dad programmed you?"

"Not exactly," Theremin replied. "Normally, I'm pretty good at everything and I can get by. But when I get *really* good at something, some of my data banks are erased. And then I have to start from scratch."

"That's awful," Newton said. "At least I'm not starting from scratch every time. I guess with me, I'm slowly building."

"So it's risky that I'm trying to ace this programming test," Theremin continued. "But I want to impress Father, since he's a programming expert. Maybe he'll be nicer to me if I make him proud, you know?"

Wow, Dr. Rozika sounds like a terrible dad, Newton thought. *Is that better than having no father at all? I mean, maybe I do have one out there, but I can't remember him, so it's like having none at all.*

His thoughts were interrupted by a scream from one of the cafeteria workers. Newton whirled around in his chair to see Peewee standing on top of the woman's hairnet.

"Oh no," Newton whispered to Theremin. "How the heck did he get out?"

"Who knows?" Theremin said. "But we have to catch him!"

Newton ran to the food line just as Peewee dove off the worker's head into a pan of oatmeal. The nutritious glop splattered the cafeteria ladies.

Nomnomnomnomnom . . . The little monster started chowing down on the oatmeal.

"Enough, Peewee," Newton said, and he picked up the monster by his furry tail, while the cafeteria worker glared at him.

"Sorry," Newton said quickly, and hurried back to his table. He deposited Peewee in the toolbox and made sure it was locked.

"Just stay put, Peewee," Newton said. "Shelly needs me to keep an eye on you."

Zzzzzzzzzzzzzzzz.

The sound of snoring answered him.

"Maybe the oatmeal calmed him down," Theremin guessed.

"I hope so," Newton said. "I don't want to disappoint Shelly."

Peewee slept through Newton's first class, History of Mad Scientists, and so did the teacher, Professor

Wagg, who was 115 years old. Peewee was still asleep at lunch, but the smell of food woke him up again. This time Newton found him on top of a pizza slice that was about to be eaten by Tootie Van der Flootin.

Newton locked him in the toolbox again, but he escaped during Genetic Friendgineering and jumped onto the Dial-Up-Your-DNA machine, accidentally turning it on. The machine zapped Debbie Darwin and changed her hair color from brown to bright orange. Professor Wells offered to reverse it, but Debbie refused.

"I've been begging Mom to let me dye my hair," she said. "She can't say no now!"

Newton stuffed Peewee back into the toolbox and headed to Dark Matter Matters class.

"You'd better stay in the box, Peewee," he whispered as he sat down. "Professor Phlegm is really strict."

With his bald head, black eye patch, long black lab coat, and black gloves, Professor Phlegm made Newton shiver with fear every time he looked at the professor.

"Settle in for a lecture, class," Phlegm announced. "It's going to be a long one."

Some of the kids groaned softly. Professor Phlegm's lectures were deadly boring. Newton checked to make sure that Peewee was in the box, and then sat back in his chair.

The sound of his own snoring woke him up a few minutes later, and he quickly sat up straight in his chair. Luckily, Phlegm didn't seem to notice Newton's nap.

He also didn't seem to notice the furry blue creature sitting on top of his bald head.

Some of the kids started to giggle. Newton stared at Peewee, horrified. Phlegm noticed.

"Is something the matter, Mr. Warp?" he asked.

"Uh . . . nothing," Newton said slowly, as he tried to figure out what to do.

Then Mimi raised her hand. "Professor Phlegm, there's a—"

"Black hole!" Newton cried. "There's a black hole in my desk!"

He jumped up and ran toward the front of the room. Everyone panicked and followed him. Newton purposely bumped into Professor Phlegm during the commotion, and Peewee tumbled off the professor's head. Newton quickly bent down, grabbed the tiny monster, and shoved him into his pocket.

"STOP THIS NOW, STUDENTS!" Phlegm thundered. "I see no black hole coming from Mr. Warp's desk. Everyone, please take your seats. Mr. Warp, please report to the office of Ms. Mumtaz."

"Okay," Newton said, relieved that his quick thinking

had worked. He grabbed his backpack and the toolbox, and hurried out of the room.

When he got to the headmistress's office, he found Shelly walking out of it.

"Newton! What are you doing here?" Shelly asked.

"Getting detention, I think," Newton answered. He handed Peewee to Shelly. "Here you go. I can't deal with him anymore."

Shelly held Peewee up to her face. "Were you a good boy, my little fuzzy wuzzy?" she asked in a high-pitched voice.

"Abldrrrrp!"

"I can tell you that means 'no,'" Newton said. "Why do you think I got sent here?"

"Oh, Newton, I'm sorry," Shelly said. "Do you want me to explain to Mumtaz that it was Peewee's fault?"

"It's all right," Newton said. "At least I got out of Phlegm's boring lecture. You picked a good day to go back home."

"I'm glad I did," Shelly said. "I learned so much! My parents said that my dad's side of the family, who changed their last name to Ravenholt, wanted to use their monster-making powers to help animals and other creatures, just like I do in the rescue lab. The original Frankenstein side wanted to create new monsters, new life."

"Is that so bad?" Newton asked.

"It can be, if you do it because you want the power and fame but don't take responsibility for what you're creating," Shelly answered. "Dr. Frankenstein did think he was advancing science, at least. That makes me feel better about playing him. If I believe the doctor was trying to do good, in some way, I can give the role more depth."

"Awesome!" Newton said. "You sound like a real actor."

"Thanks! I better get going, though. It's almost time for rehearsal," Shelly said. "See you there?"

"It depends on what kind of punishment Ms. Mumtaz has in store for me," Newton replied.

At that moment, Ms. Mumtaz called to him. "Newton, are you out there? Professor Phlegm messaged me that I should be expecting you."

Newton hurried into her office and sat down.

"Newton, what is this about crying 'black hole' in a crowded classroom?" she asked.

Newton had thought about blaming Peewee. But he didn't want Shelly to get in trouble. Watching Peewee had been his responsibility.

"Sorry, Ms. Mumtaz," Newton said. "I guess it's just been very stressful lately and I panicked. You know, after being followed around by Professor Flubitus. And then learning I'm supposed to save the school in the future, but not knowing any details."

Her cheeks flushed. "Yes, Newton, I can imagine that would be stressful. We must find a way for you to control your stress. Perhaps Theremin could help you? I recently taught him some good techniques for keeping calm."

Newton tried not to laugh, remembering his "calming" session with Theremin.

"You know what has been helping?" Newton asked. "Being in the musical. Pretending to be an Angry Villager is a great way to get rid of stress."

"Yes, I can imagine it would be," she said as the final bell for class rang. "Very well. You'd better get to rehearsal, then. But try to keep it together, Newton, okay?"

"I'll try," Newton said, and he hurried out of her office.

In the auditorium Snollygoster was instructing the students to take their seats while he made some announcements.

"Firstly, I'd like to say that I have written in a human part for Higgy," Snollygoster began. "He will be playing Dr. Fluffenstein, Dr. Frankenstein's veterinarian cousin. Higgy, you will see that I have added the scene to the script."

"Excellent. Thanks!" Higgy said.

"Now I'd like to begin with the blocking, or staging, of the musical," Snollygoster continued. "We won't be doing songs just yet. This will be like the read-through, except that I will be directing your movements onstage. Tootie, as our narrator, Captain Walton, you will be positioned on the ship's bow, over here."

He pressed a button on a remote control, and a holographic scene appeared on the stage. On one side, it looked like a ship was coming out of the wall. When Tootie moved there, it looked like she was sitting on the ship.

The main part of the stage looked like a scientist's laboratory, with stone walls, and metal racks of test tubes and strange machines. Everyone started to *ooh* and *aah*.

"The advanced hologram students are still working on it, but it's a good start," Snollygoster said. "Just a note that wherever you see holographic furniture, there is a real piece of furniture in the same spot. So you'll be able to sit in the chairs, and place things on tables."

Tootie walked over to the ship's bow.

"Shelly and Theremin, please come to the stage. Shelly, you are working late at night at your desk. Theremin, you are entering the room from the door, carrying a tray of food."

Shelly and Theremin took their places. Tootie began the narration, finishing with: "One night Dr. Frankenstein was working late in her lab."

"All right, Theremin. Now enter and bring Dr. Frankenstein the tray," Snollygoster ordered.

Theremin walked onto the stage and over to Shelly. He pantomimed putting the tray on the desk.

"Does salt this need more?" he asked.

"Stop!" Snollygoster said. "Theremin, your line is 'Does this need more salt?'"

Theremin nodded. "Right," he said. He walked away from the desk. Then he walked back and pantomimed putting the tray on it. "Does this need more salad?"

Some of the kids started laughing.

"Theremin, please try again," Snollygoster said.

Theremin placed the imaginary tray on the desk a third time. "Is this too salty?"

Snollygoster sighed. "Let's keep moving. Shelly, it's your line."

Shelly looked up from Dr. Frankenstein's desk. "*Crrrrrrooooooaaakkkkkk!*" Then her eyes got wide.

"Shelly, your line is 'The only salt I need is the salt of inspiration,'" Snollygoster said.

Shelly nodded. "*Crrrrrooooooaaaakkkkkk!*"

Then she started waving her hands and pointing to her throat.

"Oh dear," Snollygoster said. He walked over to Shelly. "Open wide, please."

He peered down her throat and then turned back to the rest of the students.

"Somebody give me Shelly's water bottle, quickly!" he said.

Newton jumped up, grabbed Shelly's metal water bottle, and handed it to Snollygoster. The professor opened it up and sniffed it.

"Vocal cord paralyzer," he said. "Shelly, someone is trying to make you fail!"

Everyone gasped. Shelly looked like she was going to cry.

"Who would do such a thing?" Mimi asked loudly.

"That shouldn't be too hard to find out," Snollygoster said. Then he called out, "Security drone!"

A drone flew down from the very top of the auditorium ceiling. Snollygoster held up the water bottle. "Play any footage involving this bottle from the last thirty minutes."

The drone buzzed, and then projected a holographic image into the air in front of them. First it showed Shelly sitting down and putting her water bottle on the chair next to her. Then Shelly turned to talk to Theremin. Behind her, Mimi unscrewed the top, used an eyedropper to add something, and then screwed the top back on.

Shelly turned around and took a big chug from the water bottle. Then the footage ended.

"It was Mimi!" Theremin cried. "Mimi tried to sabotage Shelly!"

"That footage was doctored!" Mimi yelled. "That drone's got something against me!"

The drone buzzed in response.

"Mimi, this is the second time you've attempted to use chemistry to get the role you want in this musical,"

Snollygoster said. "I'm afraid you can no longer participate."

"But—don't I get three strikes?" Mimi asked.

"This is not baseball," Snollygoster told her. "Mimi, you are out! Newton Warp, you are the new Lead Angry Villager."

Newton felt like cheering out loud, but he held it in. He didn't want to hurt Mimi's feelings, even if she might deserve it.

"I'll be back. You'll see!" Mimi cried, and then she turned and stomped out of the auditorium.

Snollygoster looked at Shelly. "I'm afraid that the paralysis will take a few hours to wear off. Let's continue with the blocking. I will read your role."

Shelly nodded, and the blocking continued. Since Theremin's part was done, he returned to his seat.

"Theremin, what happened?" Newton whispered. "You knew your line perfectly earlier."

"I'm afraid to do it right, so I'm psyching myself out," Theremin whispered back. "If I do great in this part, I could fail my programming test."

Newton shook his head. *We've got to find some way to help Theremin,* he thought. *What his dad is doing is totally unfair!*

CHAPTER 8

The Extreme Weather Challenge

"All right, everyone, put your goggles on," Shelly said, her voice back to normal.

It was Saturday, and Shelly had asked Newton, Theremin, and Higgy to meet her in the jungle for another testing session for Newton.

"What are we doing today?" Newton asked. "And why are we out here in the jungle?"

"I figured the outdoors would be the best place for today's test," Shelly said. "I got to thinking about how animals have special features that kick in when they're afraid or angry—but also, in extreme weather conditions. We haven't tested those yet."

"The weather today isn't very extreme, according to my gauges," Theremin pointed out. "Eighty-two degrees Fahrenheit, with humidity at fifty-three percent. Unusually pleasant for the tropics."

Shelly took several glass globes from her backpack.

Inside one, a snowstorm swirled.

"Those are the Micro-Weather souvenir globes," Newton said. "The ones they sell in the school store."

"Exactly. I have one snowstorm, one hurricane, and one heat wave," she said. Then she got a gleam in her eye. "And we're going to break them."

"Is that safe?" Higgy asked. "A strong breeze tends to break off bits of my protoplasm. It's quite uncomfortable."

"These things break all the time, accidentally," Shelly replied. "The effect stays within a five-foot radius, and it only lasts for sixty seconds when the weather is released. That should be small and short enough to keep us all safe, and long enough for us to test Newton's responses."

"I think I can do sixty seconds of each one," Newton said confidently.

"Great. Let's start with the heat wave," she said. "Ready?"

Newton nodded. "Ready."

Shelly smashed a globe on the grass. Immediately Newton began to feel hotter.

"Temperature jumped to ninety-six degrees, and is rising," Theremin reported.

"Newton, how do you feel?" Shelly asked. "Any different?"

Newton had jumped back to his feet. "I feel great. Energetic!"

"Do you think you might break out the snowstorm, Shelly?" Higgy asked. "I'm starting to melt."

"In five seconds," Shelly said, watching the countdown on her tablet. "Okay, next!" She broke the snowstorm globe. Snow whirled around Newton. "How do you feel now, Newton?"

"I . . . feel . . . all . . . right . . . ," he replied slowly, but his eyes were drooping. He lay down on the ground and stretched out. "Just . . . tired . . . mayyyyyyyybeeeeeeee . . ."

"Your metabolism is probably slowing down, like a cold-blooded animal's might," Shelly said. "This goes along with the lizard theory."

"His body temperature is dropping rapidly," Theremin announced. "Thirty-two degrees Fahrenheit. Thirty-one. Thirty . . ."

"What's that sprouting on his arms? And his face?" Higgy asked.

Newton looked down at his arms. White, curly hair was popping up on them. He could feel it growing on his legs and his face, too.

"Ahh! What's happening?" he asked.

Shelly reached out with tweezers and plucked one of the hairs. "I think this is wool," she said. "The curled

fibers of wool trap warm air, acting as insulation."

"Am I going to stay like this?" Newton asked.

"It looks cool," Theremin told him. "Sometimes I dream of growing a beard someday, but that will never happen. Just go with it."

"It's itchy!" Newton complained.

The storm stopped. The air around Newton got warmer. After about a minute, the wool retracted into his body.

"That was pretty impressive," Shelly said. "Ready for the hurricane?"

"I'm not sure," Newton said.

Shelly took a rope from her backpack and tied it around his ankle. "We'll all grab hold, so the winds can't blow you away."

Newton took a deep breath. "Okay. Let's do this."

Shelly broke the hurricane globe. Hurricane winds swirled and battered Newton, while his friends stayed safely outside the five-foot-wide storm area.

As soon as the first wind hit Newton, he dropped to his knees. Without knowing why, he began to dig into the dirt at superspeed. He quickly dug a small burrow in the ground, and he dove in.

Then the winds stopped.

"Wow!" Shelly said. "Newton, how did you get the idea to dig the burrow?"

"I didn't," Newton said. "I just started doing it. It was . . . automatic."

"Newton, you are even more amazing than we thought!" Shelly said, and Newton felt himself blushing. "I don't know exactly how you were burrowing so fast, but the ability saved you from the hurricane winds. This could be a trait from a rabbit or even a snake."

Newton's head was spinning. He wasn't sure if it was really cool to have all these extra abilities, or if it made him even more of a freak.

Either way, I'm really glad these guys are helping me figure this stuff out, he thought. *I'm lucky to have such good friends I can trust!*

"This is . . . a lot," he said. "I feel like I have more questions now than I did before we started."

"No pressure, but how do you feel about talking to Flubitus sometimes soon?" Shelly asked. "We'll go with you."

Newton nodded. "I guess we should. It can't hurt."

A beeping sound came from Theremin.

"That's my study alarm," he said. "Only thirty-seven hours, twelve minutes, and three point two seconds until my programming test."

"Want some help again?" Newton asked.

"For sure," Theremin replied.

"I'd help, but I need to do some research with Peewee," Shelly said. "I need to figure out how he keeps escaping from everything."

"And I'm starving," Higgy said. "I'm going to raid the kitchen's peanut butter stores before dinner."

"Then it's just you and me, Theremin," Newton said with a grin.

The two friends went to Theremin's dorm room. Theremin's only furniture was a desk and a large inflatable snowman, so Newton sat cross-legged on the floor.

"All right, Theremin," he said. "Hit me."

"Got it," Theremin replied. "Newton, use your noodle noggin!"

Newton didn't feel any different when Theremin said that. But he knew that he would when the thinking started happening.

"Ready," Newton said. "What do you need to study?"

"Third-tier coding—how to remove a given character from a string," Theremin said.

Immediately the knowledge kicked in to Newton's brain. It wasn't just that he knew the answer; he could *see* the code in his mind, the images dancing and leaping in his head like dolphins.

"First you need to convert it into a character array,"

Newton told him, "and then use a substring method to remove them from the output string."

"Character array, right!" Theremin said. "Newton, I don't know what I'd do without you. I'm so glad you're helping me. I know I'm going to ace that test on Monday."

Newton high-fived him. "You got this, Theremin!"

"I hope so," Theremin said. "It's my big chance to impress my father!"

CHAPTER 9

The Future Is Foggy

Pop! Pop! Pop!

The sound repeated through the cafeteria as students popped their lunch bubbles. The latest invention from the cafeteria staff, the bubbles floated out of the kitchen for kids to pluck out of the air, pop, and eat whatever was inside. Mumtaz had explained the plan during the morning's announcements.

"Our statistics show that you are all eating the same things day after day," she said. "These bubbles will encourage you to diversify your nutrition. The rule is, you pop it, you eat it . . . unless you have a food allergy, of course!"

Shelly plucked a bubble out of the air and popped it over her plate. A green salad spilled out all over it.

"Not bad," she said. Then she looked around. "Now I just need to find a ranch dressing bubble."

Newton popped his bubble, and hot chili poured out.

He recognized it as something he'd eaten before—and liked.

"This is fun," he said.

Around them, some kids groaned when their bubbles released lamb liver or stewed cow's tongue onto their plates. Shelly grabbed another bubble, and tomato soup splashed out, all over her salad. She sighed.

"Hmm," she said.

Newton passed his bowl over to her. "Here, we can share." He gazed around. "Where's Theremin? His programming test was last period. I wonder how he did."

At that moment Theremin literally floated into the cafeteria, thanks to the thrusters on the bottoms of his feet. He bumped into some bubbles floating around, sending chicken casserole and pizza bites cascading to the ground.

"Theremin! Good news?" Shelly asked.

"I ACED my test!" he announced, taking a seat next to her. "I can't wait to tell Father."

"That's awesome, Theremin," Newton said. "I knew you could do it."

Just then, another bubble flew in front of Shelly's face.

"Might as well see what I get," she said.

Pop!

A green powder spilled out, covering Shelly. She started to scratch herself.

"This isn't food," she said. "It's ... it's itching powder!"

Theremin spun around. "Mimi! Where are you?"

Mimi was sitting a few tables away, eating a hamburger. "Is there a problem, Theremin?" she asked innocently.

"You bet there is!" Theremin said.

"Never mind, Theremin," Shelly said. "Mimi's out of the musical, at least. I know that's bugging her worse than itching powder bugs me. I'm going to go see Nurse Bunsen for an antidote. Don't forget—we're going to talk to Flubitus before tonight's rehearsal!'

"Are you sure you're okay?" Newton asked.

Shelly grinned. "A little itching powder wouldn't get Dr. Frankenstein down, so I won't let it get me down either!"

She left the cafeteria, scratching.

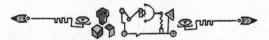

Monday night's rehearsal for the musical was scheduled for seven p.m. After dinner Newton went back to his room to change (another round of bubbles had left him splattered with broccoli soup and roast beef gravy), and

then he headed to Theremin's room.

As he approached, he could see that Theremin's door was slightly open, and voices streamed from inside. Newton paused, listening.

"I can't believe it, Father!" Theremin said. "I worked so hard to pass that programming test. I got a perfect score! And you don't even care."

"I created you to achieve perfection, Theremin." Newton knew that deep voice—it was Dr. Rozika. "Your artificial brain has infinite capabilities. I expected nothing less. You simply met my expectations."

"Fine. You expect me to be perfect," Theremin said. "Then why did you program me to fail every time I succeed? Why not let me succeed all the time? This afternoon I got a negative fifteen on my Inter-Dimensional Astronomy quiz. A NEGATIVE FIFTEEN! That's not even a real score! But that's how badly I failed."

"It is for your own good, Theremin," Dr. Rozika said calmly. "We wouldn't want things to be too easy, now, would we?"

"THERE IS NOTHING GOOD ABOUT IT!" Theremin yelled. "IT STINKS!"

"If you cannot speak calmly, then I must excuse myself," Dr. Rozika said, and left the room. In the hallway Newton stepped backward to let him pass.

Then Newton heard a loud *bam* as Theremin kicked the inflatable snowman and sent it flying out of the room. It slammed into the wall in the hallway and then began to deflate with a squealing sound.

Theremin stuck his head out the door and watched his father go. Then he saw Newton.

"Oh hey," he said. "Did you, um . . ."

"Just got here!" Newton lied. "Are you ready to go talk to Flubitus?"

"Might as well," Theremin said with a sigh.

Newton wasn't sure if he should tell Theremin what he'd heard. But he felt so bad for his friend! Theremin was hunched over as they headed through the jungle and back to the school building. Shelly was waiting for them in front of Professor Flubitus's classroom.

"Hey, guys," she said. "Here's the plan. We tell Flubitus we're not leaving until we get the truth."

"Yeah, we'll play tough," Theremin said.

"But what if he won't tell us anything?" Newton asked. "How are we supposed to get tough?"

"I . . . I don't know," Shelly admitted. "But it sounds good, right?"

Flubitus's door was open, so the friends marched in.

"Professor Flubitus, we need to talk to you," Shelly said.

"Yeah, and you're going to answer all our questions," Theremin added.

"I will do my best," the professor answered. "Please, have a seat."

They sat in seats in front of him.

"First I'd like to say that I am sincerely sorry if I was unintentionally creepy when I followed you around," Flubitus began. "I was honestly trying to protect you."

"We understand that part," Shelly said. "But we need to know why you need to protect us. Why does the future of the school depend on us—and Newton, especially?"

Flubitus shook his head. "I'm afraid I cannot tell you that."

Theremin thumped his fist on the professor's desk. "We won't take no for an answer!"

"That is the only answer I can give you," the professor replied.

The three friends looked at one another, stumped. Then Shelly spoke up.

"Well, maybe there are some things you *can* tell us," she began. "Can you give us an idea of what the future is like, in general?"

Professor Flubitus frowned thoughtfully. "I can't say much, because even the smallest thing I say might change the course of events going forward," he replied.

"But perhaps I could tell you a little bit."

"Um, does everyone in the future have green hair?" Theremin asked.

Professor Flubitus ran his fingers through his lime-colored locks. "Not really. This happened to me during an experiment gone wrong."

"Here's what I've been wondering," Shelly said. "Are there more protections for endangered animals in the future? Are monsters still considered scary and dangerous, or are they more accepted by humans?"

Flubitus paused. "I am not sure how much I can say about that, Shelly. You do play a role in the future of human and monster relations, but . . . I fear I've said too much."

"Will I ever find out where I came from?" Newton blurted out. "Will I ever meet my parents?"

Flubitus bit his lip. "Yes . . . and no," he answered slowly.

"Yes and no?" Newton repeated. "That doesn't make any sense."

Flubitus shrugged. "That's all I can say."

Newton felt tears forming in his eyes, and he brushed them away. "Can't you at least tell me if I have a family? So I know that I'm not going to be alone in this world forever?"

Flubitus paused. "I am sorry, Newton. I just can't say," he replied.

Shelly touched Newton's arm. "And you're not alone, Newton. You have us."

"What about robots?" Theremin asked. "Do people accept robots as being more like 'real' humans in the future?"

"I don't want to dash your hopes, young man," Flubitus replied. "As robot intelligence and abilities increase over the decades, the most advanced robots integrate more into human society. But they still aren't considered fully human, I'm afraid."

Theremin looked down sadly, and Newton once again felt bad for his friend.

Professor Flubitus stood up. "I don't think I should answer any more of your questions. Believe me, I understand how curious you must be. The best advice I can give you is to keep living your lives as you normally would. Things will work out in the end."

"If they work out in the end, why did you come back in time to protect us?" Newton asked.

"I suppose you could say I'm here as insurance," he said. "There is so much at stake, children. So much at stake."

Flubitus turned and gazed out the window, and Newton, Theremin, and Shelly headed to rehearsal.

They walked quietly, each one thinking about what Flubitus had said.

When they reached the auditorium, Snollygoster announced they would be staging the musical again. Tootie, Theremin, and Shelly took their places onstage. Tootie narrated the introduction, and then Theremin walked out.

"Do you want s'more salt?" Theremin said, and in his seat, Newton cringed for his friend.

Theremin tried again and again, and he couldn't get it right. "Does this need more sardines?" he said, and then tried, "This is very salty." Finally he blurted out, "Does this need more . . . soup?"

"Theremin, is there something wrong with your programming?" Snollygoster asked.

"Yes," Theremin answered. "But this is exactly how Father programmed me to be."

Newton looked over at Higgy sitting next to him, who shook his head in sympathy with Theremin. Then Newton glanced onstage at Shelly, and she nodded at him. He knew they were all thinking the same thing.

We've got to find a way to help Theremin!

CHAPTER 10

A Very Big Idea

"It's time to begin Operation: Help Theremin," Shelly said.

After rehearsal Shelly, Newton, and Higgy headed to Newton and Higgy's room, where they crawled through a vent into the tunnels underneath the school. They knew it was a safe place to meet and talk—as long as the school custodian, Stubbins Crouch, wasn't on patrol.

They had put their tablets in flashlight mode and sat on the discarded furniture in the basement—broken desks and file cabinets.

"I'm glad we're helping Theremin," Newton said. "He doesn't know, but I heard him talking with his dad. Dr. Rozika didn't even care that Theremin had passed the test."

"He treats Theremin like an experiment, not a son," Higgy said.

"And you missed what Flubitus told us," Shelly told

Higgy. "In the future, robots still aren't seen as 'real' people. Theremin looked like he was gonna cry."

"But the worst is that he's failing everything now that he passed his programming test," Newton said. "He can't even get his one line in the play right. It's not fair!"

"It's the way his father programmed him," Higgy said.

"That's it!" Shelly cried. "Maybe we can reprogram him!"

"Wouldn't we need to be programming geniuses to do that?" Newton wondered.

"You can be a genius when you use your noodle noggin," Shelly said.

As soon as she said that, Newton started seeing computer code flash through his mind.

"Maybe," he said. "But even when my noodle noggin kicks in, I don't know everything. We're going to need more help."

"First we should see if Theremin even wants to be reprogrammed," Higgy pointed out.

"We can talk to him in the morning," Shelly suggested.

Suddenly a huge shadow loomed in front of Shelly. Newton instinctively blended in with the wall behind him.

"Abbbbllllldrrrrp!"

The shadow turned out to be Peewee. The little

monster scrambled up Shelly's leg.

"Peewee, I left you locked in my room," Shelly said. "What are you doing here? Bad boy!"

"*Abbbllllldrrrp!*" This one sounded more like a growl. Then . . . *Boop!* Peewee disappeared!

Shelly gasped. "He teleported! He's a teleporting monster! How cool! That explains how he's been able to escape from every place I've left him."

Then her face fell. "Oh boy. I have my work cut out for me now." She took a deep breath. "But we've got to help Theremin, too."

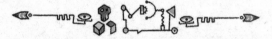

The three of them cornered Theremin in his room the next morning and told him their plan.

"Reprogram me?" Theremin asked. "You mean, fix it so that I don't stink at everything when I get good at something?"

"We're going to try," Shelly said. She held up a flash drive. "First we need to download a copy of your existing program, so we know what we're dealing with."

Theremin pointed to the port on the side of his head. "Go for it."

Shelly inserted the flash drive, and removed it when the download finished a few minutes later.

"What next?" Theremin asked.

Newton piped up. "I was thinking we could get some expert help in the Brain Bank. Your programming knowledge and my noodle noggin might not be enough."

"Sounds good," Theremin said. "But when should we do that? We're all busy with rehearsal."

"We've got a free night on Wednesday," Higgy said. "How about then?"

"Perfect!" Shelly said. "Let's start in the library after dinner on Wednesday, and then move on to the Brain Bank. We can do this!"

She held out her hand. Newton placed his on top of hers. Higgy placed a squishy, gloved hand on top of Newton's. And Theremin put his robot hand on top.

"Operation: Help Theremin!" they cheered.

"I have failed at everything I've tried to do since Monday," Theremin complained, when they met in the library on Wednesday night. "It's never been this bad. I don't know a proton from an electron from a lardon."

"I think one of those is bacon," Higgy said.

"I don't even know!" Theremin cried.

One of the library drones quickly flew up to him. "Quiet, please."

"We'd better keep it down. Those drones can be tough," Newton said, remembering a time when a swarm of drones had ejected him from the library.

"All right, so first thing we need to do is to find some robotic programming books and check them out," Shelly instructed. "Then we'll see what we can learn in the Brain Bank."

They scanned the shelves and found some books. Then they headed to the Brain Bank. Newton got a little chill when he walked inside. He always thought of it as the place where he had been born. That's where Shelly and Theremin had found him on the first day he could remember anything.

"Hey, Theremin, remember that first day we met and you were downloading one of the brain's data directly into your head? And then it went splat against the wall when you disconnected?"

"Yeah, that was pretty funny," Theremin said.

Pffft! Pffft! Pffft!

Higgy moved around the shelves in the room. Each one contained a jar with a brain in it.

"Who are we looking for?" he asked.

"An expert in robotics programming, if we can find one," Shelly said.

Higgy pointed to a brain. "What about Leonardo da

Vinci? Didn't he make the first humanoid robot?"

"Did he?" Shelly asked. "I didn't know that."

"I did," Theremin said. "He's a legend in the robot world."

Higgy nodded and added, "He built a robot knight in the fifteenth century. It could walk and sit down and even move its jaw, and probably moved on a pulley system. That was advanced at the time, but it won't help much with computer programming."

"Good point! But I'm going to download his data anyway, just in case his brain can help," Shelly said. She inserted the cord coming from da Vinci's brain jar into her tablet, and downloaded the data. "Anybody else?"

"We could try Ada Lovelace," Higgy answered. "She was the first person to publish a computer algorithm."

"Got it," Shelly said, connecting her tablet again. "Higgy, how do you know all this?"

"I'm a bit of a coding nerd," Higgy admitted. "I love computers. When we were helping Theremin study, Newton's noodle noggin did most of the work, so I kept quiet."

"We're going to need all the help we can get to reprogram Theremin," Shelly said. "Now that we've got all this data, we should plug it into the mainframe computer in the programming lab."

Theremin shook his head. "Father's always in there. If he found out what we were doing . . ."

"I believe I have a solution," Higgy said. "Follow me."

They left the library and followed Higgy into the boys' dorms and into Newton and Higgy's room. Higgy began to toss aside all the junk on the floor.

"I'm excited that you're finally cleaning up, Higgy, but we need to help Theremin," Newton said.

Higgy tossed aside one more mound of clothes and then turned to the others and said, "Ta-da!"

Clearing away the mess had revealed an enormous computer setup, with two huge towers and three monitors.

"Whoa," Theremin said.

"Her name is Abigail," Higgy said. "I brought her from home, and named her after my favorite aunt, who got me my first holo-book about coding when I was three. I haven't needed her here yet because we have our tablets. Here, let me plug her in."

Abigail came to life with the sound of hums and beeps, and filled a wall of the room.

"*Hello, Higgy,*" she said in a digital-sounding voice. "*How may I help you?*"

"This is awesome," Shelly said. "So, what's our first step?"

"First we download Theremin's data into Abigail," Higgy replied. "We're going to have to isolate the character string that Dr. Rozika used. Finding that won't be easy, but I can work on it. Once we find it, we can use my expertise

and Newton's noodle noggin to try to change it."

"In the meantime, I'll read the programming books we got," Newton said.

"I'll translate the da Vinci transfer on my tablet and see if there's anything helpful there," Shelly offered.

"And I can take a look at the Ada Lovelace download," Theremin said. "Even though I'm bad at everything else, I'm still good at programming."

"Awesome! We have a plan!" Shelly said. "Let's get to work."

They studied the material until bright moonlight shone through the window and they were all yawning.

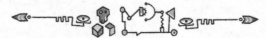

The next day Higgy kept Abigail running, working on finding the code in Theremin's program. After a long day of classes and a rehearsal for the musical, they worked late again on Thursday night.

"Abigail estimates that we can isolate the code strand in about thirty-three hours, if I keep her running," Higgy reported after they'd decided to stop for the night.

"That brings us to Saturday," Shelly said. "Then we move on to phase two. Theremin, maybe we'll have you fixed by Monday!"

"Isn't Monday tomorrow?" Theremin asked.

"No, tomorrow's Friday," Shelly said.

"But Friday was yesterday," Theremin said. "That's when they served French fries in the cafeteria."

Shelly and Newton looked at each other. Theremin's intelligence fail was worse than ever!

"Theremin, I have an idea," Shelly said. "I think you should leave the programming to us for now. You're really good at it, but it's making things worse for you."

"Whatever you say, Shelly," Theremin said, and Newton thought he sounded grateful.

Newton patted him on the back. "Don't worry, Theremin," Newton said. "We got this."

"Thanks, Newton," Theremin said.

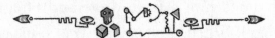

Over the next few days, Shelly, Higgy, and Newton were busy. When they weren't at class or rehearsal, they were working on Theremin's programming. After Abigail isolated the character strand that caused Theremin to lose intelligence after he succeeded at something, Newton and Higgy tried to remove it without causing any other hiccups in the code.

By late Sunday night, they were close. Newton's noodle noggin was racing, and Higgy's gloved hands were flying over the keyboard. Shelly was leaning against the boys' bunk, dozing with Peewee on her lap.

"Eureka!" Higgy cried suddenly, waking Shelly.

"Did you get it?" she asked.

"I think so," Higgy replied. "Newton, use your noodle noggin and check."

Newton scanned the code characters quickly. He didn't know how, but he understood them perfectly.

"I'm pretty sure this is right," he said.

"Abigail, what do you think?" Higgy asked.

"The probability that you have fixed the code is ninety-five percent," she replied.

"That's good enough for me," Higgy said. "Shelly, a flash drive please."

Shelly handed him a flash drive and Higgy plugged it into Abigail. When the transfer was finished, and he handed the flash drive back to Shelly, his glove slipped off. Some of the goop got onto the flash drive. He quickly wiped it off.

"Here you go," he said. "Good as new."

"May I rest now, Higgy?" Abigail asked. *"I have been working very hard for days."*

"Thanks, Abigail," Higgy said, powering her off.

Shelly looked at the flash drive. "Everyone, let's meet at Theremin's room early in the morning," she said. "Tomorrow he'll be a brand-new robot!"

CHAPTER 11

Ahoy, Scallywags!

"Will it hurt?" Theremin asked early the next morning as Shelly prepared to upload his new programming.

"Nope," Shelly replied. She inserted the flash drive into Theremin's head, and then wiped her hands on her leggings. "Sticky!"

Theremin's eyes flashed red, then green, then blue. Alarmingly, his head began to spin around.

"I think something's wrong!" Newton said.

But then Theremin's head stopped spinning. His eyes returned to normal.

"Hey," he said.

"Hey, Theremin," Shelly said. "How do you feel?"

"Fine," he replied.

"Theremin, what's the difference between a proton and an electron?" Higgy asked.

"Protons and electrons are in the center of an atom," Theremin replied. "Protons have a positive charge, and electrons have a negative charge."

Higgy let out a cheer. "Hoorah! It worked."

"It really looks that way!" Newton said, and he felt so happy for his friend. Now Theremin could finally have a regular life!

Shelly looked at the time on her tablet. "Hey, we should get to breakfast so we have time to eat before class starts."

As they hurried to the cafeteria, Newton noticed something about Shelly.

"Where's Peewee?" he asked.

"I left him with Professor Yuptuka," Shelly said. "She's an expert on teleporting, and she's got him in a cage with a force field that prevents it. I need to create one of my own so I can keep Peewee safe when I can't keep an eye on him."

"Cool," Newton replied.

They were late for breakfast, so they stopped at the smoothie machine. Newton was making himself one with extra energy, because he'd been up so late, when he heard a strange noise behind him.

"*Woof! Woof! Woof! Woof!*"

He turned. Theremin was barking like a dog.

"Theremin, are you okay?" Newton asked.

Then Tori Twitcher walked by, and Theremin started

to growl. He began chasing Tori, who screamed and jumped up on top of the smoothie machine.

Shelly grabbed Theremin by the arm. "Down, boy."

She pulled Theremin out into the hallway, and Newton and Higgy followed.

"Theremin, stop acting like a dog!" Shelly said.

Theremin's eyes flashed green, and his head spun around again.

"What do you mean?" Theremin asked.

"You don't want to bark? And growl? And chase cats?" Shelly asked.

"Why would I?" Theremin replied.

Shelly, Higgy, and Newton looked at one another.

"Maybe it's just a little glitch," Higgy said. "He sounds fine now."

Newton wasn't so sure that Theremin *was* fine, but he didn't say anything. *I'll stick close by him today,* he thought, and it was a good thing he did.

In History of Mad Scientists class, Professor Wagg asked if anyone knew the ancient code of the mad scientists. Theremin raised his hand and answered.

"E-thay only-ay rue-tay isdom-way is-ay in-ay owing-knay ou-yay ow-knay othing-nay!"

Everyone started to giggle. Wagg raised a furry white eyebrow.

"That is correct, Theremin. The only true wisdom is in knowing you know nothing . . . but please do not answer me in pig latin!" he said.

Shelly looked at Newton and raised her eyebrows.

In Electro-Fluid Physics class, Professor Maskawa asked if somebody could name the parts of a neuron, and Theremin raised his hand again.

"Four, seven, three, five, thirty-six!" he replied confidently.

"Um, no," Professor Maskawa said.

"Seventeen, twelve, eight," Theremin muttered.

Shelly and Newton looked at each other again.

It got worse as the day went on. In Genetic Friendgineering class, Theremin began to cluck like a chicken and walked around the room, flapping his arms.

In Dark Matter Matters, he hopped onto the particle accelerator and pretended he was riding a horse.

"Yee-haw, pardners! Time to ride away on the lonesome prairie!"

Professor Phlegm scowled at him. "The only place you'll be riding away to is detention," he said, and Shelly pulled Theremin away.

"I think he believes he's a cowboy," Higgy whispered to Newton.

"Something's wrong," Newton replied. "We've got to get him back to the room and hook him up to Abigail."

But right after class they had practice for *Frankenstein: The Musical*. Snollygoster clapped his hands as everyone entered.

"Today we're going to rehearse the big musical number in act two," he announced. "'Monster, Go Home!' Every cast member will be singing in this one, so please come to the stage."

Newton got up and then looked around. "Hey, where did Theremin go?"

"Ahoy, scallywags!"

Newton looked up. Theremin was dangling from a cable attached to the ceiling! He swung down onto the stage.

"Shiver me timbers! The seas be mighty fierce today!" he cried. "Nonetheless we must set sail, for adventure awaits!"

"Mr. Rozika, I applaud your enthusiasm, but please save your pirate performance for another production," Snollygoster said. "Now, please take your place behind the Angry Villagers!"

Theremin kept singing things like, "Batten down the hatches," and, "All hands on deck," instead of the words for the songs. Luckily, everyone was singing really loudly, so Snollygoster didn't notice.

When practice finished, Newton grabbed Theremin's hand and motioned for Shelly and Higgy to follow. "Come on, dude. We need to go check on something with Abigail."

"Aye, Captain!" Theremin replied cheerfully.

A few minutes later Newton, Shelly, Higgy, and Theremin were gathered around Abigail. Shelly had downloaded a copy of Theremin's programming onto a flash drive again, and Higgy had uploaded it to Abigail to analyze. After just a minute, she spoke.

"This file is corrupted, Higgy."

"Blimey!" Theremin wailed.

"Rats!" Higgy said. "Abigail, do you know the cause of the corruption."

"Let me do a quick diagnostic," Abigail replied. *"Okay, I'm done. I am 99.9999999 percent certain that the file was corrupted by protoplasm."*

Everyone looked at Higgy.

"Some of my goo must have dripped onto the flash drive," he said. "I'm sorry, guys. I'm not sure how to fix this now."

"I know one person who can fix this," Newton said. "But he might not want to help us."

"You don't mean . . . ," Shelly began.

Newton nodded. "Dr. Rozika."

CHAPTER 12

Father and Son

"Come on, Theremin," Higgy said. "Let's go hunt for treasure in the basement."

"Aaargh!" Theremin replied.

Shelly and Newton made their way to Dr. Rozika's lab in the main building.

"I know this is a crazy idea," Newton said. "But we made Theremin even worse than before! We have to talk to his dad."

Shelly sighed. "I know. I just don't like that guy."

They found Dr. Rozika in his lab, his bald head shining in the light of his computer monitor. He didn't turn as Newton and Shelly called out to him.

"Um, excuse me, sir?" Newton asked.

Nothing.

"Dr. Rozika?" Shelly tried.

Dr. Rozika spun around in his chair. "What is it? Can't you see I'm working on something that's very, very important?"

His pale skin stretched tightly over his thin frame, and his cold blue eyes made Newton shiver. *He seems less human than Theremin!* Newton realized.

Shelly answered the doctor. "We have something very, very important to talk to you about: Theremin."

"Oh, has he been bothering you?" Dr. Rozika asked. "No problem. I will discipline him."

"No, we're his friends," Newton said.

"Nonsense! Theremin has no friends! He has no need of friends," Dr. Rozika said.

"Yes, he does," Shelly insisted. "He has feelings and emotions. You should know. You gave him those."

"Yes. Well, unfortunately, emotions are all the rage in the field of artificial intelligence these days," Dr. Rozika said. "I wanted to leave them out, but my colleagues would have accused me of slacking. Although, I may have gone overboard. The boy doesn't seem to know how to control them!"

Hearing Dr. Rozika call Theremin a boy gave Newton some hope. Was there a chance that Dr. Rozika really did think of Theremin as a son, and not just an invention?

"Well, he needs your help now, and it's our fault," Shelly continued. "We tried to change his programming, and—"

"You what?" Dr. Rozika's eyes flashed with anger,

reminding Newton of how Theremin's eyes flashed sometimes. "That's tampering with my property!"

Newton forgot how afraid he was of Dr. Rozika and spoke up. "Theremin isn't anybody's property," he said. "He's our friend, and he asked us for help. Once he started doing great in programming, he failed at everything else miserably."

Dr. Rozika nodded. "Exactly as I programmed him to."

"How would you feel if you failed at everything every time you did something well?" Newton asked.

"That would never happen," he argued. "I have never failed at anything!"

"But don't you see, this isn't *fair*!" Shelly protested. "It makes Theremin feel bad about himself. He gets really sad."

Dr. Rozika clicked his tongue. "Those terrible emotions again. Perhaps I should remove them."

"No!" Newton said quickly. "Theremin's perfect the way he is. Except for what we did to him."

"And what did you do to him?" Dr. Rozika asked.

"We tried to get rid of the programming that makes Theremin fail," Shelly replied, "but it didn't work. There was a glitch."

Dr. Rozika grinned smugly. "Of course there was. I built in a system to garble the coding for language and behavior if anyone tried to change Theremin's original programming."

"So it wasn't Higgy's goo at fault!" Newton said. *He'll be relieved.*

"And I suppose you want me to fix your mess?" Dr. Rozika asked. "I must admit, I'm curious to know how my garbling worked out."

"See for yourself," Shelly said, and she held out her tablet. She had recorded some of Theremin's pirate antics.

"Yo, ho, ho! Don't try to hornswoggle me, ye crusty old landlubber!" Theremin was saying. Then he shook his fist.

Dr. Rozika's face softened. "Hornswoggle . . . landlubber . . . my goodness, does he remember?"

"Remember what?" Newton asked.

Dr. Rozika typed into his keyboard, and a picture of him appeared on the screen. He was welding Theremin's head, and in the background a cartoon pirate was on his monitor.

"When I was creating Theremin, it was a great strain on my mental energy, and I took to—how do you young people say it?—bilge-watching?"

"Binge-watching," Shelly corrected him.

"That's right, binge-watching," Dr. Rozika said. "I binge-watched all five seasons of the *Billy the Pirate*

cartoon while I worked on constructing Theremin's body."

He scrolled through the screen. "See? There are his little robot feet. And there are his cute little hands."

"Um, yeah, cute," Newton said, and he glanced at Shelly. Was Dr. Rozika softening?

Dr. Rozika turned back to Newton and Shelly. "Theremin must have downloaded all Billy's pirate lingo into his memory banks. I had no idea," he said. "Those were good times."

Then he snapped out of his memory and began to glare at Shelly and Newton again. "Please bring him to me, so I can fix him."

"And can you fix him so that he doesn't fail at things anymore?" Newton asked.

"Just bring him here," Dr. Rozika said firmly.

Shelly and Newton came back with Higgy and Theremin a few minutes later.

"Ahoy, Father!" Theremin called out.

"Ahoy, Theremin!" Dr. Rozika replied. "Come here, Son, and let's get you fixed up. You'll be seaworthy in a jiffy."

Higgy looked at Newton with questioning eyes, and Newton raised a finger to say *Shh!* and mouthed the words: *I'll explain later.*

Meanwhile, Dr. Rozika plugged a cord into a port in Theremin's head. Theremin's eyes flashed red, then blue, then green. His head spun around and then stopped.

"Say something, Theremin," Dr. Rozika said.

"Something," Theremin replied.

"Very funny," Dr. Rozika said. "Please say something a little more, so we can see if we're okay."

"Father, fine am I," Theremin said.

"Don't you mean, 'I am fine, Father'?" Dr. Rozika asked.

"Said I what exactly is that," Theremin replied.

"He's saying everything backward!" Shelly realized.

Dr. Rozika's pale face turned beet red. "That—that's impossible," he said. "I just fixed the glitch!"

"I guess you failed," Newton said without any hint of meanness. "I bet that doesn't feel very good, does it?"

"No, it feels awful! I have never failed before, and I plan to never do so again," Dr. Rozika said, and then he paused. "Ah, I see."

"Making you proud is the thing Theremin cares about most," Shelly told him, "and the thing he most wants to succeed at."

"True is that," Theremin agreed.

"And if he keeps failing at everything, that's only going to make *you* look bad," Shelly went on, taking another angle. "If you fix him, you'll both be happier."

"I suppose you are right," Dr. Rozika said. "Leave him with me. I should have him fixed by the morning."

Newton, Shelly, and Higgy looked at one another, unsure if they could trust Dr. Rozika. Would he make Theremin better, or even worse? They had to hope he was capable of really changing, and staying true to his word. He was their last option.

They waved good-bye to Theremin and said they would be back tomorrow.

"Tomorrow you see!" he replied.

The next morning they raced back to Dr. Rozika's lab before breakfast.

They found the scientist and the robot arguing.

"Now that I have updated your programming, Theremin, I expect straight As from you this semester," Dr. Rozika was saying sternly. "There are no more excuses!"

"But, Father, that's not fair!" Theremin replied. "I've already got failing grades in all my classes except computer programming."

"You are a Rozika! Pull yourself up by your bootstraps and find a way!" Dr. Rozika thundered.

"But that's impossible!" Theremin cried.

"Nothing is impossible! Every mad scientist knows that, Son," Dr. Rozika said.

Theremin smiled when his father called him "Son."

"Yeah, I'll remember that," Theremin said. "Ahoy . . . Dad."

"Ahoy, Theremin," Dr. Rozika said.

Rozika seemed just as mean as ever, but something had shifted between him and Theremin. There was a . . . tenderness that Newton hadn't seen before. Newton felt another pang of jealousy. *I don't care if my parents are mean mad scientists, or robots, or pirates, or aliens from outer space,* he thought. *I just want to know who they are!*

"So, how do you feel, Theremin?" Shelly asked as they left Dr. Rozika's lab.

"Better than ever!" Theremin replied. "I'm going to have to work pretty hard to get my grades back up, but at least I know I won't fail now no matter what I do. Failing because I didn't learn enough doesn't sound so bad, but failing because I was programmed to fail was horrible. Although it's going to be pretty tricky to get straight As with practice for the musical almost every night!"

"Yes, but at least you'll be able to ace your line now," Higgy said.

Theremin nodded and declared in a booming voice: "Does this need more salt?"

CHAPTER 13

Frankenstein: The Musical!

For weeks Newton and his friends worked hard practicing for the musical. They were so busy rehearsing and doing schoolwork that they put aside the idea of testing Newton's abilities, and that was just fine with him. Nothing weird or scary happened, and he hadn't freaked out or camouflaged since the last time they'd tested him.

Now it was opening night, and everything was ready. The robot orchestra could play perfectly in tune, the holographic sets looked stunningly real, and the kids working the special effects created fake lightning flashes and thunder that both looked and sounded like the real thing. The actors all knew their lines . . . except for Theremin. He was trying to say his line under his breath while they waited for the show to start.

"Does this need more soap?" he tried, and then, "Does this need more salsa? *Ugh!* Does this need more sassafras?" Theremin bowed his head.

"Theremin, what's wrong?" Newton asked. "I thought your dad fixed you."

"He did," Theremin replied. "Now I'm nervous! I'm going to be onstage, in front of all those people! I keep thinking that I'm going to mess up, and that makes me mess up!"

Newton gripped the robot's metal shoulders. "You've got to snap out of it, Theremin. You've been doing your line perfectly for weeks. Scan your memory banks and you'll see."

Theremin's eyes flickered as he scanned his memory. He nodded.

"You're right, Newton," he said, and then he tried saying his line a few times in different ways. "Does this need more *salt*? Does *this* need more salt? Does this *need* more salt? I think the first one's the best. Hey, I'm good at this acting thing!"

Newton high-fived him. They were standing backstage with the rest of the cast. Theremin was dressed in a chef's coat and hat, and Newton wore a lace-up shirt and brown pants, which was supposed to make him look like an old-timey villager.

Shelly walked up to them, wearing a long lab coat, rubber gloves, and goggles.

"I can't believe today's the day!" she said. She glanced

at the curtain. "The audience is filling up out there. My parents said they were coming. I'm really excited."

"Dad said he can't make it. He's busy working on a new creation," Theremin said with a hint of sadness in his voice.

Well, at least you have a father, Newton thought, and then he felt bad for thinking it. He was happy Theremin and his dad were getting along better, even if he was jealous. And he didn't need any parents watching him perform, he told himself. *I've got my friends, and that's enough.*

Professor Snollygoster came backstage wearing a purple crushed-velvet suit with a yellow shirt with ruffles down the front. He clapped his hands.

"Students, I want you to know how proud I am of how hard you've all worked," he began. "Now I want you to go out there and bring the story of Dr. Frankenstein to glorious life. The whole school is watching!"

"Okay, now I'm feeling nervous again," Theremin whispered to Newton.

"Don't worry, Theremin," Newton said. "Everything's going to go great!"

"Tootie, Theremin, and Shelly, take your places, please!" Snollygoster announced.

Tootie moved to the bow of the ship, dressed in a blue coat with fancy buttons and a tricornered hat. Shelly sat

down at Dr. Frankenstein's desk, and Theremin waited behind the door with a tray of food covered by a silver dome.

The lights dimmed, and Newton could hear the audience quiet down. People started to clap as the holographic curtain dissolved, revealing Tootie behind it. She launched into the introduction.

"I'll never forget the day I found the doctor, floating in the middle of the ocean on a small boat. I invited her onto my ship, and asked to hear her story. She told me her name was Dr. Frankenstein . . . and the story she told me is one I shall never forget."

The stage lights shone on Shelly pretending to furiously write notes at her desk. Theremin stepped out onto the stage, carrying the tray. He stopped in front of Shelly, removed the dome, and then froze.

Oh no, Theremin! What's wrong? Newton thought, and then he followed Theremin's gaze to see that the robot was staring at something in the audience. It was Dr. Rozika! He was sitting in the front row, his bald head almost shining under the glare of the stage lights. *His dad came after all!* Newton realized. *Come on, Theremin, you can do it!*

The audience was quiet, waiting for Theremin to speak. He composed himself.

"Does this need more salt?" he asked Shelly.

Shelly pushed her chair back and looked up at him. "The only salt I need is the salt of inspiration!" she told him.

Then she launched into a song.

"Inspiration!
It's giving me consternation!
I don't need a standing ovation.
All I need is inspiration!"

Shelly sang and danced her way across the stage, and when her song finished, the audience burst into loud applause.

Mimi must be hating this, Newton thought, and he searched for her in the audience, but didn't see her.

After the applause died down, Higgy walked onstage, in his human role. He had decided to transform his goo into a human shape to play Dr. Fluffenstein, a trick Newton had seen him do before. Higgy looked like an adult man made of green goo, wearing a lab coat decorated with a pattern of illustrated puppies and kittens.

"Hello, Cousin," he said in a posh British accent.

"Well, if it isn't my cousin Dr. Fluffenstein, the famous veterinarian," Shelly said. "What brings you here?"

"I've got a problem with one of my cat patients that I think you can help me with," Higgy said. "He thinks he's a dog."

"He does?" Shelly asked.

"Yes," Higgy said. "You could say he's very *purr*-plexed!"

Higgy delivered the joke perfectly, and the audience laughed.

"I don't have time for silly games, Cousin," Shelly said. "I am working on something very important!"

"I'm working on something important too," Higgy said. "I am creating a cross between a cocker spaniel, a poodle, and a rooster."

"Now, *that* sounds interesting," Shelly said. "Tell me more."

"I call it a cocker-poodle-roo!" Higgy said, crowing like a rooster, and the audience cracked up. "My next creation will be a cross between a dog and a frog," Higgy continued. "I call it a croaker spaniel!"

The audience groaned, but Dr. Rozika chuckled loudly.

"Enough of your jokes, Cousin," Shelly said. "Now maybe—"

"*Abbllldrrrrp!*"

Peewee popped up, seemingly out of nowhere, and landed on Higgy's gooey head! Shelly stared at him, her mouth open, but she quickly came up with a plan.

"It looks like one of your patients has escaped,

Fluffenstein," she said. "You'd better get going and let me think in peace."

"I'll go, but may I borrow an umbrella?" Higgy asked. "It's raining cats and dogs out there!"

Everyone laughed and clapped as Higgy left, and Newton high-fived him when he came offstage. Newton's friends were doing great!

I just hope I do great too.

He anxiously waited for his time to go onstage. First he watched Tori Twitcher meow her way around Dr. Frankenstein's office. He watched Rotwang sing his song about being an assistant. He watched Odifin and Shelly argue about science and how to create responsibly.

Then the lights dimmed, and the scene changed from Dr. Frankenstein's lab to the village. Newton and the other Angry Villagers walked out onto the stage. Seeing all the faces in the audience staring at him made him break out in a sweat.

Keep it cool, Newton, he told himself. He took a deep breath and began.

"Dr. Frankenstein is up to something strange in that castle. I just know it," he said.

"Yes," Debbie Darwin agreed. "I see strange lights at night."

"And I hear strange noises," Boris Bacon added.

"Well, I won't let her put this village in any danger," Newton said, and then the lights went dim again.

Newton ran offstage, his heart pounding. Theremin and Higgy were waiting to high-five him.

"Great job, Newton," Theremin said.

"Thanks," Newton said. "And we're just getting started. I can't wait until act two!"

During intermission the cast stretched, changed costumes, drank water, and sang scales to keep their voices limber. Newton spotted Shelly wandering around the stage.

"What did Higgy do with Peewee?" Shelly asked.

Professor Yuptuka walked up. "I've got him, Shelly," she said, holding up a glass box with Peewee inside it. "Sorry about that. I didn't use a strong enough field the first time. This little guy is quite a determined teleporter."

Shelly tapped on the cage. "Thanks, Professor. I guess he's a star now. Right, Peewee?"

The little creature turned his back on her and sulked in the corner. Shelly put the cage on a crate. "Just wait here for me until I'm done, okay?"

"*Abblllddrrrp!*"

Then Snollygoster's voice rang out. "Everyone, get ready for act two."

"Break a leg, Shelly," Newton said. "You're doing great!"

"Thanks, Newton," Shelly said.

She took her place onstage, and Higgy climbed onto the table in the lab. Act two began with a big scene: the Monster coming to life.

The curtain dissolved and the audience quieted down, and Shelly began her speech.

"The moment has finally come. . . ."

"*Abblllddddrp!*"

Newton spun around just in time to see Peewee scurrying across the floor.

"Oh no!" he hissed. "Peewee, you're going to ruin Shelly's scene!"

Newton dashed after Peewee. The little monster scurried behind one of the thick, velvet curtains. Newton followed him there—and ran into Mimi!

"Mimi? What are—" Then he noticed the souvenir weather globe in her hand, holding a tornado, and his eyes got wide.

"Don't try to stop me, Newton," Mimi said, holding up the globe. "In ten seconds I'm going to lob this onstage. The tornado will blow Shelly away, and then *I'll* blow everyone away when I take over the role as Dr. Frankenstein. The show must go on, right?"

"Don't you dare, Mimi," Newton said. "Shelly earned that role fair and square. Just give me the globe and I

won't tell anybody, I promise."

"Nice try, Newton," Mimi said. "But I need my moment in the spotlight, and I'm going to get it."

"Abbllddrrrp!"

Peewee teleported to the top of Mimi's head. Startled, Mimi dropped the globe. Newton lunged for it. He grabbed it with his sticky hands, but his own force sent him tumbling out onto the stage.

This time he knew it was happening but still couldn't stop it: He camouflaged to match the stone wall of Dr. Frankenstein's lab. The audience gasped. Shelly turned around, startled. She quickly came up with a line that would help make it seem like Newton had disappeared on purpose.

"I have been working far too long without sleep," she said. "I must be seeing things!"

Newton ran offstage, his heart pounding. *Everyone saw me camouflage! Everyone in the entire school!*

He returned to his normal appearance, and Theremin zoomed over to him. "Newton, what happened?"

"Have you seen Mimi?" Newton asked. He held up the globe. "She's trying to get Shelly out of the play."

Then they heard Mimi's voice. "Stop it! Stop it! Get off me!"

They followed the sound, and saw that Peewee was

making a nest in Mimi's hair. Snollygoster approached.

"What is all this?" he hissed. "Higgy's big number is coming up."

Newton held up the globe. "Mimi was trying to sabotage Shelly."

"I was—ow!" she cried, as Peewee yanked a strand of her hair.

"I see," Snollygoster said. He pressed a button on his watch, and four security drones zipped in from nowhere. They grasped Mimi and flew away. Peewee jumped off her head and landed on Newton's shoulder.

Onstage, Higgy was beginning his song, and the audience listened, rapt.

"What do you see when you look at me?
A monster, a creature, a beast?
When you see me, why do you flee?
Give me a chance, please, at least."

When Higgy was done, Newton would have to go onstage and be an Angry Villager again. His palms started to sweat. Theremin put a hand on his shoulder.

"It's going to be okay, Newton," Theremin told him.

"But everybody saw me camouflage!" Newton said. "Everybody knows I'm different!"

"And is that really so bad?" Theremin asked.

Newton paused. Theremin was different, and he had

a dad and friends and had aced his line in the play. Newton's friend Higgy was made of green goo, and he was onstage singing with a beautiful voice.

"You want me to run,
You want me to hide.
But you're scared of my looks.
You can't see what's inside."

"Maybe I'm a monster too," Newton said. "For all we know, I could be. But maybe . . . maybe being a monster's not so bad."

"That's the spirit!" Theremin said. "Now get ready for the big number."

Newton forgot about being different. He went out onstage with the rest of the cast and shook his fist and stormed the castle. He sang "Monster, Go Home!" badly, and at the top of his lungs, with all the emotion Snollygoster could want.

The villagers chased Higgy from the castle. Dr. Frankenstein left and sailed the world looking for her creature. The musical ended with Tootie on the ship.

"I dropped off Dr. Frankenstein on an island, and I never saw her again," Tootie said. "But somehow I know that her name . . . her name will be remembered, and she will be known throughout history as the greatest mad scientist who ever lived!"

The lights dimmed, and the audience went wild. They applauded and rose to their feet. Then the cast came out and took a bow. Newton ran out with the Angry Villagers, his heart pounding with happiness, not nervousness. But he heard some kids and adults in the crowd saying things like: "How did Newton do that?" and "What's up with Newton?"

When everyone in the cast took a bow, Ms. Mumtaz came onto the stage.

"I just want to thank Professor Snollygoster and the cast for all their hard work," she said. "And also, everyone who helped backstage. Let's hear it for our robot orchestra, and for our holographic projection team!"

The audience clapped.

"Finally, I'd like to thank our special effects department," she said. "They're responsible for the amazing effects we saw tonight, such as the teleporting blue monster, and our incredible camouflaging villager."

Everyone clapped again, and Newton breathed a small sigh of relief. He had accepted that he was different, and that was fine. But maybe it was better that his secret wasn't out—at least not yet.

The curtain closed, and Newton and the rest of the cast went backstage. Everyone cheered and hugged one another.

"That was a close call," Shelly told Newton.

"Yeah, but it worked out," Newton said.

Tori Twitcher ran up to them. "Snollygoster is throwing us a cast party in the cafeteria!"

"I'll be there in a few minutes," Shelly said. "I want to go see my parents."

"Mine came too," Higgy said. "I'll catch up with you all later."

"And I want to say hi to my dad," Theremin said.

His three friends left, and Newton felt a little deflated. Then Boris ran past him and punched him in the shoulder.

"Let's go to the party, dude. Villagers rule!" he cried.

"Sure, I'll be right there," Newton said.

He had suddenly felt a familiar prickle on the back of his neck. He turned to see Professor Flubitus standing there.

"Are you following me again?" Newton asked.

"No, I came to talk to you," Professor Flubitus said. "I've been thinking about what you said about wanting to know if you had a family. About being alone in the world."

Newton waited expectantly.

"Well, I think it's only fair for you to know that you're not alone, Newton," Professor Flubitus said. "You have

a relative . . . right here at Franken-Sci High!"

Newton held his breath. He wasn't sure if he'd heard Flubitus right.

"A . . . a relative?" Newton repeated.

Flubitus nodded. "I can't tell you who it is. You'll have to figure it out for yourself."

Then, with a guilty look, the professor hurried off.

Newton stood still, thinking. He wasn't sure if he could trust Flubitus. *But if it's true, that means . . . that I definitely have family,* he thought. *I'm not alone!*

Soon after, Theremin floated over to Newton. "There you are! Everyone's waiting for you in the cafeteria."

"What? Oh, thanks," Newton replied, and he followed the robot out of the auditorium and up to the crowded cafeteria, where Higgy was making a group of kids laugh with farting noises, Peewee was teleporting from Shelly's left hand to her right, and Tootie Van der Flootin was tossing slices of pizza into the air and kids were jumping up to catch them.

Flubitus might be lying, he thought. *But that's okay. Because here at Franken-Sci High, I'm never really alone!*

Why does Odifin become a giant brain?
Who will win at Trivia Night?
Don't miss the next book about
Jim Henson's™
FRANKEN-SCI HIGH

Jim Henson's
FRANKEN-SCI HIGH
BEWARE OF THE GIANT BRAIN!

CREATED BY MARK YOUNG
ILLUSTRATED BY
MARIANO EPELBAUM

"Students of Franken-Sci High! It has come to my attention that many of you are still asleep after last night's cast party. Please report to the cafeteria right away. The school has an important announcement to make!"

Newton Warp groaned as he woke up to the voice of Headmistress Mumtaz, which seemed to be shouting into his ear. Then he felt something tickle the inside of his ear. A tiny, mechanical, fly-like creature flew out of it and left the room through the crack on top of the door. It was quickly followed by another mechanical fly that came from the bottom bunk, where Newton's roommate slept.

Newton hung upside down from the top bunk and gazed at his roommate, Higgy, who was oozing out of bed. His gooey green body, made entirely out of protoplasm, was tucked inside a pair of flannel pajamas with rubber chicken drawings on them.

"Why is she making us go to the cafeteria?" Newton moaned. "It's the weekend!"

"You know Mumtaz," Higgy replied. "She loves an assembly."

Newton hopped off the bed. "And why was that announcement so loud? It felt like it was right in my ear."

"Oh, those are her fly drones," Higgy explained. "She has a whole horde of them that she can target to reach each student at the school. Each one has a powerful micro speaker inside. Pretty impressive, but usually they're reserved for emergencies."

"Well, I need more sleep," Newton said with a yawn. "I hope this announcement is worth it."

"We'd better get dressed before she sends her screaming cyborgs," Higgy warned. "They're a lot louder!"

Newton knew that listening to Higgy was a good idea, and he slipped on jeans and a lime-green T-shirt with the school's motto on it: "A Brain Is a Terrible Thing to Waste . . . Unless You Can Grow Another One."

He yawned again. It wasn't just that he'd been

up last night, celebrating with the rest of the cast of *Frankenstein: The Musical.* Even after he'd climbed into bed, well after midnight, he hadn't been able to sleep. His mind had been racing with the news he'd heard earlier that night.

Newton was a new student at Franken-Sci High. The school was filled with plenty of unusual students: robots, Higgy, and even a kid who was a brain in a jar, Odifin Pinkwad. Newton looked like an ordinary human, but he was probably the most unusual student of them all.

His friends Shelly and Theremin had discovered him in the Brain Bank of the school library with no memory of who he was or where he'd come from, with a school ID with his name on it, and a bar code permanently imprinted on the sole of his left foot.

In the last few weeks, Newton had learned some things. He had uncovered strange memories of being hatched from a giant egg. He had extra-human abilities: his fingertips and toes were sticky and helped him climb walls; he could camouflage himself when he was in danger; he could sprout gills and breathe underwater; and he could make himself look like other humans if he wanted to.

He had also learned from Professor Hercule Flubitus

that he and Shelly were very important to the future of the school, but Professor Flubitus hadn't told them why. Even so, they were so important that Flubitus had traveled from the future to protect them.

And last night Flubitus had told Newton the most amazing thing of all: Newton had a relative living at the school! When Newton has heard this, he'd been shocked and quiet. But the more he thought about it, the more he wanted to scream and jump and laugh and cry all at the same time. Shelly and Theremin and Higgy were awesome friends, but it still bothered Newton that he had no idea where he was from, or even if he had a family. Professor Flubitus's news was the best news ever.

But the flustered professor had refused to give up the identity of the relative to Newton. And Newton had gone to the cast party, where they'd eaten lots of pizza and freeze-dried potato chips, and had danced and sung songs from the school musical, and it just hadn't been the place to talk about what Flubitus had said. So Newton had been up all night, wondering who this relative might be.

Was it one of the students? Would it be somebody nice, like Tori Twitcher? Or somebody not so nice, like Mimi Crowninshield?